COVENTRY LIBRARIES

Please return this book on or before the last date stamped below.

To renew this book take it to any of
the City Libraries before
the date due for return

Coventry City Council

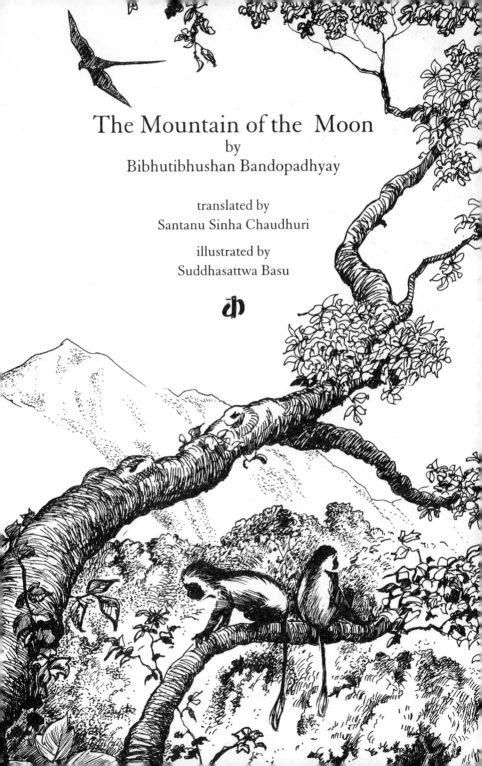

The Mountain of the Moon
by
Bibhutibhushan Bandopadhyay

translated by
Santanu Sinha Chaudhuri

illustrated by
Suddhasattwa Basu

KATHA

KATHA
A-3 Sarvodaya Enclave
Sri Aurobindo Marg
New Delhi 110 017
Phone: 2652 4350, 2652 4511
Fax: 2651 4373
E-mail: kathavilasam@katha.org
Internet address: www.fictionindia.com

KATHA is a registered nonprofit society
devoted to enhancing the pleasures of reading. It works in the fields of
story, storytelling and story in education.
KATHA VILASAM is its story research and resource centre.

Cover design: Sujasha Dasgupta and Taposhi Ghoshal
Cover and inside illustrations: Suddhasattwa Basu
Series editor: Geeta Dharmarajan
In house editors: Shoma Choudhury, Gita Rajan
Production coordinator: Sanjeev Palliwal

Typeset in 11.5 on 15 pt ElegaGarmnd BT at Katha
Printed at Usha Offset, New Delhi

Distributed by KathaMela, a distributor of quality books.
A-3 Sarvodaya Enclave, Sri Aurobindo Marg, New Delhi 110 017

Katha has planted two trees to replace the tree that was used to
make the paper on which the book is printed.

ISBN 81-87649-30-5

1 3 5 7 9 10 8 6 4 2

For Khuku

Bibhutibhushan Bandopadhyay
Barrakpore, Jessore
18 September 1937

Preface

Chander Pahad is neither the translation of an English novel nor is it based on any foreign work of fiction. The storyline and the characters of this novel are creations of my own imagination.

However, in order to make the geographical details and descriptions of different natural regions of Africa realistic, I have taken help from travelogues written by Sir H H Johnston, R Forbes and some other well-known explorers.

It may be relevant to mention here that the Richtersveldt Mountain described in this novel is a well-known mountain system of Central Africa and the myths of Dingonek (the Rhodesian Monster) and Bunip are prevalent in the jungles of Zululand even today.

St Franco's Prayer to the Sun used in this novel was translated by late Mohini Mohan Chattopadhyay.

Barrakpore   Bibhutibhushan Bandopadhyay

Jessore

18 September 1937

This is the author's Preface to the original Bangla volume of *The Mountain of the Moon* which was first published in Bangla as *Chander Pahad* in 1937.

ONE

The year was 1909. Five years before the First World War. Young Shankar had just come back home after finishing school in Calcutta. He spent his days chatting with friends, enjoying his afternoon siesta, and fishing in the village lake in the evenings.

After a month had been spent like this, his mother called him and said, "Shankar, you know your father's not well. How will you continue with your studies? Who will pay your college fees? Perhaps it is time you looked for a job."

His mother's words set Shankar thinking. His father had been ill for the last few months and it had become difficult for him to meet Shankar's expenses in Calcutta. But what could Shankar do? Who would offer him a job? He did not know anyone who could help.

Finding a job in those days was not all that difficult. One of their neighbours worked in a jute mill some distance away from the village. Shankar's mother requested his wife to ask her husband to help Shankar find a job at the mill. The next day, the kindly gentleman came over to say that he would try his best to help Shankar.

Now Shankar was no ordinary boy. He was the best sportsman in his school. Once he had won the first prize for high jump in a district meet. He was the best centre forward around and a champion swimmer. Besides, he was also an expert boxer and horse rider. And he was very good at climbing trees too. However, with all these activities, he hadn't done too well in his studies and had managed only a second division.

But there was one subject in which he had remarkable knowledge. Geography. He loved to read books on geography and would study any map that he could lay his hands on. He knew almost all the constellations that can be seen from our part of the world – the Orion, the Great Bear, the Cassiopeia, the Scorpion, and so on. He knew the months of the year they could be seen in and their precise orientations. He could spot them easily in the night sky. Without doubt, there weren't – and still aren't – many boys in our country who knew so much about these things.

This year, when he came back from Calcutta after the exams, Shankar brought home a number of such books and maps. He has been studying them quietly and pondering over them. No one knows where his thoughts wander ... In the meantime, his father had taken ill, his family had fallen on hard times and now his mother wanted him to take up a job. What should he do? He could not bear to see his parents suffer. He had no choice but to join a jute mill, although such a course would shatter his dreams forever. It would be a disgrace if the best centre forward, the district high jump champion and the well-known swimmer ended up as a paan-chewing jute mill babu. When the siren shrieks in the morning, he would scamper to the factory, tiffin-box in hand, return home in the afternoon for a quick meal and set off again. And his day would end with yet another shrill hoot at six in the evening. Shankar's young mind refused to even think of such a future. His whole being rebelled at the idea. Would a racehorse have to pull rickety carriages?

That evening, Shankar sat alone by the riverside, thinking. His heart wants to fly away to far, faraway places … in the midst of a hundred daring adventures. Like Livingstone and Stanley, like Harry Johnston, Marco Polo and Robinson Crusoe. Since his childhood he has prepared himself for such a future. But he has never stopped to think that what was possible for boys from other continents could not even be imagined by boys from our country. They are destined only to become clerks, teachers, doctors or lawyers. The desire to set off for the unknown is for them but a distant dream.

Later that night, Shankar read from the hefty volume of Westmark's Geography in the dim light of the earthen lamp. One section of the book particularly fascinated him. It was a description by the famous German traveller Anton Hauptmann, of his experience of climbing a massive mountain in Africa – Chander Pahad, the Mountain of the Moon. He has read it so many times. And every time he has imagined himself setting off, like Herr Hauptmann, to conquer the Mountain of the Moon …

That night he had a strange dream … He is in a dense

jungle of tall bamboo grass. Not too far away, wild elephants are trampling down bamboo stems. He is climbing up a huge mountain along with another person. The spectacular views around them are exactly like Hauptmann's description of the Mountain of the Moon. The same dense jungle of bamboo stalks and tall trees bedecked with creepers. Underneath, a thick carpet of sodden leaves and occasional barren patches of hard rock. And far away, visible through gaps in the foliage, the snow-clad mountain peak washed by moonlight. A clear sky with a few stars scattered around. He seems to hear the trumpeting of wild elephants. The whole jungle shakes with the sound.

It was so vivid. Shankar woke up, as if with the noise, and sat up in bed. Early sunlight was streaming in through the window.

Oh! What a dream! Do early morning dreams really come true? Many people say so!

There was an old, derelict temple in their village built by a famous zamindar long ago. Now the temple was in ruins with peepal and banyan trees growing from its cracked cornices. But the roof over the altar was intact. Although there was no idol in the temple, the local people performed puja there every Tuesday and Saturday and women put vermilion and sandalwood paste on the altar. People had great faith in the presiding deity of the temple. The wishes made here were fulfilled.

Shankar took an early bath that morning and went to the temple. He hung a pebble on an aerial root of a banyan tree in front of the temple and prayed for something.

In the evening he went there again and, for a long time, sat quietly on the untended grass in front of the temple. Although it was not far from the village, the place was full of wild plants and shrubs. Nearby was an old, abandoned building that was believed to be haunted. Normally, no one visited the place alone. But Shankar enjoyed the quiet solitude of this desolate, rundown temple compound!

The early morning dream had left a deep imprint on his mind. As he sat in that wilderness, he once again recalled the trumpeting elephants crushing bamboo stalks. The snow-clad peak washed by moonlight seemed to stand as a silent sentinel of a faraway dreamland! Many a dream had he dreamt in the past, but none of them had been so vivid. Never had a dream made such an impact on him …

But it's only a dream, just make-believe! The real Mountain of the Moon will always be too far away for him. Could a mountain of the moon ever come down on earth? He would have to work as a clerk in a jute mill. That was his destiny, wasn't it?

But such strange things happen in our lives! If you read them in fiction, you would laugh them off as absurd. In Shankar's life too, such a turnaround came about, from a totally unexpected quarter.

The next day, shortly after he had returned from his morning walk by the riverside, his neighbour Rameshwar Mukherjee's wife came to him with a scrap of paper in her hand.

"My dear Shankar," she said, "at last there's news of my son-in-law. He has written to his people at Bhadreshwar. Pintu came back from their house yesterday. This is the address they have given. Could you please read it out to me?"

Shankar said, "Oh! It's been almost two years since you heard of him. How he had scared all of you by running away without a trace. Hadn't he done the same thing once before?"

He unfolded the piece of paper. On it was written,

Prasaddas Bandopadhyay,
Uganda Railway Head Office,
Construction Department,
Mombassa, East Africa.

The paper fell from Shankar's hand. East Africa! Can anyone run away that far? But he knew that this person, Nanibala Didi's husband, was a strong-willed, adventurous man who loved to wander about. Shankar had met him once when he had come to their village. Shankar was in school then. Prasad was a generous and well-read person, but could not stick to a job for long. Once earlier, he had run away to Burma or Cochin or somewhere. Shankar knew that this time too, he had had an argument with his elder brother and had left home. And gone all the way to East Africa!

Rameshwar Mukherjee's wife had no idea how far that could be. After she had left, Shankar noted down the address and wrote to Prasad immediately. Does he remember Shankar from his in-laws' village? He has completed his schooling and is yet to be employed. Could Prasad Da please look for an opening for him in his rail company? He is prepared to go anywhere.

After one and a half months, when Shankar had given up hope, he received an envelope. The letter read,

No 2, Port Street
Mombassa

Dear Shankar,

I have received your letter. I do remember you. I can hardly forget that I lost to you in arm-wrestling. Will you come here? Please do. If boys like you don't come out, then who will? A new railway track is being laid here. The company requires many people. Come here as soon as you can. I take the responsibility of getting you a job.

Yours,
Prasaddas Bandopadhyay

Shankar's father was very happy to see the letter. In his youth, he too had had an adventurous bent of mind. He did not like the idea of his son joining a jute mill, but, because of financial difficulties, had been forced to give in to his wife's wishes.

A month later, Shankar received a telegram from

Bhadreshwar. Prasad had come home. He would return to Mombassa in twenty days. Shankar could accompany him if he wanted to.

TWO

Four months later. End of March.

The branch line of the rail road from Mombassa to Kisumu-Victoria Nayanza lakes was being laid at that time. This place was three hundred and fifty miles to the west of Mombassa. The Noodsberg station of Uganda Railways was seventy two miles to the southwest. Shankar had joined the construction camp as a clerk cum storekeeper and, like everyone else, was staying in a tent as no houses or cottages had yet been constructed. The camp, set up on a clearing, had tents pitched in a circle. The grassland around the camp was a vast plain of tall grass – some as tall as a man, some even taller – stretching to distant horizons, with a few trees scattered around. Close to the tents, right at the edge of the clearance, was a baobab tree, the famous baobab of Africa. Back home, Shankar had seen pictures of the baobab, now he could not get enough of the real.

Shankar's young and enthusiastic mind seemed to have found the fulfilment of his dreams in this remote wilderness of Uganda. Everyday, as soon as he finished his work, he went out for long walks in whichever direction he felt like – east, west north or south.

One day, the chief engineer in charge of the construction camp called him and said, "Listen, Ray. You shouldn't go out alone like this. You shouldn't even step out of the camp unarmed. Firstly, you might lose your way in the grasslands. In these parts, there have been instances when people have lost their way and died of thirst. Secondly, Uganda is the land of lions. Right now the lions may have moved away because of the clamour and clatter of our tools, but one can never trust them. Be very careful. This area is not at all safe."

One afternoon, while work was on in full swing, a sudden, loud scream was heard from the grassland nearby. Everyone, including Shankar, ran towards the direction of the scream. They searched the grassland thoroughly. There was nothing to be found.

Who had cried?

The engineer sahab arrived. A roll call of the workers was taken. One of them was missing. On enquiry, it was found that the man had gone towards the grasslands a little earlier on some work. No one had seen him coming back.

After searching for some more time, a lion's pugmarks were spotted on the sandy ground nearby. The engineer sahab took a rifle and, along with a large group of people, followed the marks. Far away from the camp, behind a big rock, they discovered the bloodstained body of the unfortunate man but there was no trace of the lion. The hue and cry raised by the men had made it run away, leaving its prey behind. The injured man was carried back to the camp. He died before evening.

The very next day, a wide area around the camp was cleared by cutting down the tall grass. For some time, the campers talked of nothing but lions. Then, in about a month's time, the incident started fading from people's memory. Things went back to normal.

One night, a big fire of twigs and straw was roaring in front of the workers' huts. It had been a very hot day but it turned chilly shortly after nightfall. The men were all sitting around the fire and chatting. Shankar too was there, listening to the chatter and reading the Kenya Morning News by the light of the fire. The newspaper was five days old. Yet, in these desolate grasslands, it was his only window to the world beyond.

Shankar had made good friends with Tirumal Appa, a Tamil clerk. Tirumal, a boy of Shankar's age, spoke English and was a spirited soul. He had run away from home in search of adventure. Today, sitting next to Shankar, he had been talking through the evening of his village, his parents and his younger sister whom he was extremely fond of. Of all his family members, he missed his sister the most. He was planning to go home towards the end of September. Won't the sahab grant him leave for two months?

The night gradually deepened. The fire was becoming dim from time to time and the men were adding dry sticks to keep it going. Many of them got up and went off to sleep. It was quite late when the crescent new moon showed up lazily near the horizon. The vast prairie was covered with the hide and seek of

light and darkness and the tall, dark shadows of the wild trees.

Shankar watched the splendour of the still, silent night of this faraway, alien country with a strange feeling. He leaned back on a tent post and observed the extraordinary beauty of the endless, desolate savannah before him. Many a thought crossed his mind. Beyond that baobab, the unfamiliar country stretched up to Cape Town. In between, there were many mountains, jungles, the pre-historic ruins of the city of Zimbabwe, and the vast and terrifying Kalahari Desert – the land of diamonds, the land of gold!

A famous prospector stumbled upon a stone and fell down. He picked up the stone and observed it closely. He found traces of gold in it. A major gold mine was discovered at that place ... Back home in India, he had read so many stories like this.

This is Africa, that mysterious continent, that land of gold, the land of diamonds. No one knows how many unknown tribes, landscapes and species of animals are hidden in its endless tropical rainforests.

Shankar had drifted off to sleep, thinking of all these things. Suddenly there was a sound and he woke up with a start. The moon was high in the sky and the stark white moonlight was as bright as daylight. The fire had died out completely and the

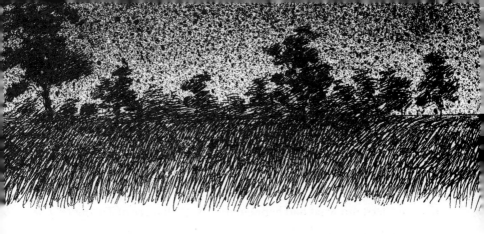

workers, huddled together near the fire, were fast asleep. There was complete silence all around.

Shankar's gaze turned to the space next to him, where Tirumal had been sitting and chatting. Where was he? Perhaps he had returned to his tent.

Shankar too was about to get up and go to his tent when a loud roar was heard from the field to the west. In the soft moonlight, the tents seemed to tremble with the awesome roar. The workers woke up with a jerk. Engineer Sahab came out with his rifle. This was the first time Shankar had heard a lion's roar. In this vast, unending grassland – where words like Distance and Direction lose their meaning – drenched in the late night moonlight, the roar evoked an indescribable feeling in Shankar's heart. Not fear, but a mysterious, complex feeling.

There was an elderly Masai worker in the camp. He said the nature of the roar indicated that the lion had killed someone. It would never have roared like that if it had not killed a man.

Tirumal's friend, who shared his tent, came and said that Tirumal's bed was empty, that he was not in their tent. The news alarmed everyone. Shankar himself went into Tirumal's tent and found it empty. Immediately the workers lit torches, picked up rods and went out in search of Tirumal. They looked into each tent and called out his name but no one answered.

They then looked closely at the place where Tirumal had been sleeping. There were signs of a heavy object being dragged over the ground. It didn't take long for everyone to understand what had happened ... A small piece of Tirumal's shirt was found under the baobab tree. Engineer Sahab followed the trail, Shankar by his side and the others following them. They searched far and wide around the camp till late into the night, but could not find Tirumal. The lion roared again, this time from far away. It sounded like the frightful cry of the reigning demoness of that deserted plain.

The elderly Masai said, "The lion is moving away with its kill. But we shall have to suffer a lot because of it. It would make life miserable for us. It would not stop before killing or wounding many more people. Beware! Once a lion starts eating humans, it becomes extremely cunning."

By the time they returned to the camp, it was three in the morning. The moonlight was still bright and the grassland was lit clearly. In this part of Africa, not many birds can be seen during the day, but at night, an unearthly sweet warble of some unknown bird can be heard. Shankar could hear the same bird trilling from the branches of a faraway tree, saddening the heart. He did not want to go to sleep immediately although the rest of the people, tired after the midnight expedition, had gone into their tents. Before retiring, however, they had lit a large fire. After a while, Shankar too went into his tent. There was no point in being reckless. But he watched the mysterious moonlit grassland through the window of his tent.

A strange feeling came over him. Perhaps Tirumal's fate had dragged him all the way to Africa for just such an untimely death. He wondered why his own destiny had brought him here!

Africa is fascinatingly beautiful, but she is dangerous! Though she looks like the acacia filled fields of Bengal, Africa can be an unknown deathtrap. Death has placed its unexpected, cruel traps everywhere, no one can say what will happen the next moment.

Africa has accepted the first sacrificial offering – the Hindu youth, Tirumal. She wants more!

After Tirumal's death, life in the camp became unbearable because of the lions. A man-eating lion is a dangerous animal as it is both cunning and daring. Not just after sunset, it became impossible to go out alone even during the day. In the evenings, huge campfires were lit in a number of places around the camp. The workers sat close to the fires where they chatted, cooked and had their dinner. During the night, Engineer Sahab went round the camp a couple of times with his rifle and fired shots in the air. But despite all precautions, a worker was taken by a lion one evening, barely two days after Tirumal's death.

The next day, a Somali man went out to crush stones only three hundred yards from the camp ... he did not return.

It was after ten o'clock that night when Shankar was coming back from the engineer sahab's cottage. There was hardly anyone outside as the workers had retired early. The fires had almost died out. Jackals were howling far away. The howls always reminded Shankar of his village in Bengal. He closed his eyes and tried to imagine he was home and the hog

plum tree in their courtyard was just round the corner. Today too, he stopped for a moment and closed his eyes.

What a wonderful feeling. Where was he? Was he in his house lying on a cot next to the window? Would he see the leaves of the hog plum when he opened his eyes? Could it be true? Should he open his eyes?

He opened his eyes slowly.

The grassland was dark. In the faint starlight, at a distance, the baobab stood like a demon. Suddenly he felt as if something was moving on the umbrella shaped, low thatched roof of a hut in front of him. The next moment he froze in terror and shock!

A huge lion was digging through the thatched roof with its forepaws. Once in a while it was putting its snout into the hole, to smell something.

The hut was at the most ten yards from him. Shankar knew he was in grave danger. The lion was busy making a hole through which it would enter the hut and pick up its victim. It was too busy to notice Shankar. No one was outside. Fearful of lions, everyone stayed indoors at night. Shankar was totally unarmed. He did not even have a stick.

Shankar fixed his eyes on the lion and started walking backwards towards the chief engineer's cottage. A minute … two … he did not know he had so much control over his nerves. Not a sound escaped his lips, nor did he try to turn around and run.

He lifted the curtain of the sahab's door and entered the cottage quietly. Engineer Sahab, still working at his table, was surprised at Shankar's behaviour. But before he could ask anything, Shankar said, "Sahab! Lion."

The chief engineer jumped out of his chair, "What? Where?"

There was a .375 Mannlicher rifle on the gun rack. The sahab took it down and gave Shankar another rifle. They came out of the cottage quietly. The hut with the circular roof was close by. But where was the lion? Shankar pointed his finger and said, "I saw it just now, sir! It was trying to dig through the thatch."

Engineer Sahab said, "It's fled. Wake everyone up!"

In a short while, a big commotion broke out in the camp. The workers picked up rods, pickaxes and clubs and left their huts and tents with a loud uproar. They made a big racket and started searching. A hole was indeed seen in the roof of the hut. The lion's pugmarks too were seen, but the lion had made off. They made the fires bigger by putting in more twigs and straw. Many of them did not sleep well that night but hardly anyone stayed outdoors.

Shankar had just fallen asleep late in the night when he woke up to the sound of people shouting. In that din, he could make out the Masai workers screaming, Simba, Simba, over and over again. There were two gunshots. Shankar came out of his hut and asked someone what the matter was. The lion had attacked and wounded a mule in the stable, that's all. Everyone in the camp had dozed off towards the end of the night when this mishap occurred.

The next evening, a young worker was killed within a hundred yards of the camp. Within four days, another man was taken from under the baobab tree.

People were too scared to go out to work. Men working with pickaxes on a railway line had to walk long distances in small groups. Now they refused to go far from the camp even during the day. The camp was not safe at night either. Fear had got into everybody. Everyone thought it would be his turn next. There was no certainty any more. Work could hardly go on in such an atmosphere. Only the Masai workers were unmoved. They were afraid of nothing, not even the Lord of Death. They were the only ones to go two miles away from the camp with their pickaxes. The chief engineer visited the site with his rifle a couple of times during the day to see if things were all right.

Despite a number of protective steps, they could not get rid of the lions. Many attempts were made but no lion could be shot. Some people said that there were a number of man-eating lions, not one. How many of them could be killed? But the engineer sahab said that not many lions were man-eaters. All the damage was being done by only one of them.

One day, the sahab asked Shankar to take a gun and visit a site where a pickaxe team was working. Shankar requested the engineer sahab to give him his Mannlicher.

The sahab agreed and Shankar took off on a mule. There was a watering hole about a mile away from their camp. By the time Shankar could see this pond, it was three in the afternoon. No one was around. The scorching sun had baked the ground and the hot air was shimmering near the horizon.

All of a sudden, the mule stopped and refused to move ahead. Shankar felt it was scared to walk towards the watering hole. After a while, there was a movement in a nearby bush but Shankar could not see what it was. He got off the mule, but still it refused to move forward.

Suddenly, lightning seemed to streak through Shankar's body. Was a lion waiting in the bush? He had heard that lions tracked their prey silently, from behind bushes, and attacked at an opportune moment. What if it was so? Shankar felt it was unsafe to move ahead. He decided to go back. The moment he turned the mule towards the camp, something moved in the bush again. A huge tawny animal jumped upon the mule with a loud roar. Shankar was a few yards ahead of the mule. He turned around and quickly fired his gun twice. He was not sure if he had hit the lion, but the mule was on the ground and the tawny animal had disappeared. Shankar went up to the mule and found a large chunk of flesh torn off its shoulder. The ground was red with blood and the mule was thrashing around in pain. Shankar fired a shot to end its suffering.

He returned to the camp. The sahab said the lion must have been hurt. It could not be easy for the lion if a heavy bullet had hit it. But had it actually been hit? Shankar said he could vouch no such thing. He only knew he had fired the shots. The men in the camp searched carefully for the next few days, but couldn't find a dead or injured lion.

Towards the beginning of June the rains came. The camp was withdrawn from the place partly due to the lion-menace and partly because the rains and the marshland nearby made the place unhealthy.

Shankar did not have to stay again in a construction camp. He got a job as the stationmaster of a small station thirty miles from Kisumu and left with his belongings.

THREE

Shankar reached his railway station around three in the afternoon. With a new job under his belt, he got off the train in a happy frame of mind. The small station building and the platform made of packed earth were fenced with barbed wire. His room was behind the station. It was small, almost a pigeonhole. As the train left for Kisumu, Shankar felt as if he had landed up in the middle of an endless ocean.

Never ever in his life had he imagined such a lonely place.

He was the only employee at the station. There was not even a porter. He himself was the porter, signalman and stationmaster ... all rolled into one. These small stations were not profitable yet and were in the process of being tried out. The railway company did not want to spend too much on them. There was one train in the morning and one that had left just then – there was no other train the rest of the day.

Shankar, therefore, had a lot of spare time. He just had to take over the charge of the station, that's all. The outgoing stationmaster was a Gujarati and knew quite a bit of English. He made tea for Shankar and himself. The gentleman was very happy to see Shankar. It seemed he had had no one to talk to for quite some time. The two of them strolled from one end of the platform to the other as they talked.

"Why have they put up these barbed wire fences?" Shankar enquired.

"Oh! That's nothing," the Gujarati gentleman replied. "This is a remote place … that's why."

Shankar felt the man was trying to hide something, but did not press further. In the evening the stationmaster made chapattis and called Shankar for dinner. While eating, he suddenly exclaimed, "Oh no! I forgot."

"What happened?"

"There is no drinking water. I forgot to take it from the train."

"What? Don't you get drinking water anywhere around here?"

"No. Nowhere. There is a well, but its water is very bitter and brackish. You can only wash utensils with it. The company supplies drinking water by the train."

What a place! No drinking water, no human beings. Shankar wondered why they needed a station here at all.

The former stationmaster left the next morning. Shankar was now all by himself. He did his personal chores, cooked, ate and went to the platform when it was time for the trains to come. In the afternoon he either read, or slept on the large table in the station room. In the late afternoon, when the shadows lengthened, he walked on the platform.

The station was surrounded by a vast, endless savannah with tall grass jungles dotted with cedar and acacia trees. Far away, a mountain range could be seen along the horizon. It was a beautiful place.

Before leaving, the Gujarati gentleman had asked Shankar not to venture into the grassland. Shankar had asked him why. He had not received a clear answer then. But one night, he got it from a very different source.

Late that evening, after he had had his dinner, Shankar was in the station room writing his diary ... he would sleep there itself, on the table. The door to the room had glass panes and was shut, but not bolted. On hearing a faint noise, Shankar looked up and saw a huge lion on the other side of the door, standing with its snout touching one of the glass panes. Shankar froze. The slightest nudge and the door would open. He was totally unarmed. There was only a wooden ruler on the table.

The lion, apparently with some curiosity, observed Shankar and the kerosene lamp on the table. It stood there quietly for some time. Not for long, maybe two minutes at the most, but Shankar felt they had both been looking at each other for an eternity. Then the lion seemed to lose interest and moved away. Shankar regained his senses, rushed to the door and bolted it quickly.

Now he understood why there were barbed wire fences around the station. But he had made a slight mistake, he had not understood the reasons fully. He had to wait for a few days for the complete answer.

That came from a different quarter.

The next morning Shankar narrated his encounter with the lion to the guard of the train. The guard was a nice person. He heard Shankar out patiently and said, "The situation is the same everywhere in this region. There's another station twelve miles down the line. There too, the same problems. And at this station ..."

He was about to say something, but stopped midway and hurriedly boarded the train. After the train started moving, he shouted, "Be very careful. Be careful at all times!"

Shankar became very worried. What were these people trying to conceal? Could there be something besides lions? Anyway, from then on he took the precaution of lighting a fire in front of the station room every evening. He entered the room well before dark, read or wrote his diary till late into the night.

The nocturnal experience was strange. Darkness descended on the vast plain around the station, a strong night wind rustled through the branches and leaves of the cedar tree on the platform, jackals howled through the night and sometimes lions could be heard roaring at a distance. It was indeed an amazing life.

This was the life he had wanted. This was in his blood. This desolate place, these mysterious nights, this sky full of unknown stars, this apprehension of danger ... *this* was life. A safe and protected life may be that of a clerk, not his.

One day, after signalling off the afternoon train, Shankar was about to enter his kitchen when he stepped back swiftly on seeing something on the post. A huge yellow cobra, with its hood open, was stretching almost two feet away from the post.

Had Shankar noticed it even two seconds later ...

But how was he to get rid of the snake? The next moment the snake climbed up the post and vanished inside the thatched roof of the hut. Shankar was in a fix. He had to go into the hut to cook his food. His adversary was not a lion for him to shut the door and light a fire outside. After hesitating for a while, he decided to enter the hut. He cooked and ate his dinner hurriedly and went to the station well before dusk. But there was nothing to prevent snakes from entering the station room too!

When the train arrived the next morning, a new porter got down from the guard's compartment with Shankar's ration. The company sent rice and potatoes from Mombassa to these remote stations twice a week. The cost was recovered from the employees' salary.

The porter was a Gujarati from India. After putting the sack down, he looked at Shankar in a strange manner. Then he rushed back to the train, as if he wanted to avoid the questions Shankar was about to ask him.

Shankar noticed the way the man had looked at him. It seemed there was a mystery attached to the place that no one wanted to share with him, as if they were under instructions not to reveal it. What was the matter?

Two days later, he almost stepped on a snake while entering his quarters. It was a yellow cobra. It could have been the same snake, it might have been another.

Later that day Shankar carefully examined the floor of his quarters and the surrounding area. There were large rat holes and cracks everywhere – in his courtyard, on the kitchen walls, in the packed earth platform. There were holes and heaps of dug up dirt everywhere. But still he did not grasp the significance of these.

One night Shankar was asleep in the station room. It was quite late in the night and pitch black. Suddenly he woke up, as if for a moment he had been endowed with a sixth sense that alerted him of an impending danger. He shivered with a strange kind of fear. Why couldn't he find the torch even after groping for it? What was that indistinct sound in the room. Suddenly his hand touched the torch. Like a robot he turned around and switched it on. Immediately he froze in terror and amazement and sat like a statue on his bed with the torch in his hand.

Between him and the wall, temporarily dazzled by the sudden light, was the most deadly and venomous snake of Africa, the black mamba. The snake was standing on its tail with its hood about four feet above ground. This is not surprising, the black mamba chases people and usually bites them on the shoulder! Shankar had heard that coming away alive after an encounter with a black mamba was like getting a new lease of life.

One of Shankar's natural strengths was that he could remain calm in a crisis, that he did not lose control over his nerves. He realized that the moment the light slipped off the snake's eyes, it would come out of its trance and strike. His life depended on holding the light resolutely and steadily on the snake's eyes, without the least movement. He would be safe as long as he could do this, but if his hand trembled even slightly ...

Shankar held the torch with a steady hand. The snake's eyes were like two sparkling beads of light. The tremendous power and fury of the snake could be seen in its black, lithe

body, as sharp as a whip ... Shankar has become oblivious to the station room and its furniture, the continent of Africa, his job with the railways, the rail line from Mombassa to Kisumu, his country, his family – the entire world seemed to have emptied out and condensed into the two beads of light ... there was nothing else beyond that. Darkness. Empty, like death.

The only thing that existed was the ferocious, venomous snake. The snake that could inject fifteen hundred milligrammes of deadly poison through its fangs. And was waiting to do just that ...

Shankar's arm became numb, his fingers went to sleep. How long could he hold the torch? Maybe, the two beads of light were not the eyes of a snake, maybe they were fireflies or stars ... or ...

Were the torch cells weakening? The shaft of white light was turning yellow and lifeless ... But the fireflies and the stars were glowing as before. Was it day or night? Would morning come after sometime? Or was it going to be night?

Shankar controlled himself. The burning gaze of those eyes had hypnotized him. He had to remain alert. Even if he screamed, there was no one to come to his rescue in this endless wilderness. He knew that his life depended on the strength of his nerves. But he could not go on any longer. His arm was aching badly and had gone completely numb. How much longer would he have to hold the torch? Let the snake bite him, he wanted to rest his arm.

The wall clock struck three times in a row. Perhaps Shankar's life had to end sharp at three o'clock because his hand shook with the chime. The beads of light vanished. But where was the snake? Why hadn't it struck?

In a flash it occurred to Shankar that like him the snake too had been hypnotized. This was his only chance ... He jumped off the table, shot out of the room like lightning and closed the door behind him.

He spent the rest of the night on the platform. The next morning, when the train arrived, he explained the situation to the guard. The guard went to see the station room along with Shankar.

There was no sign of the snake. The guard said, "You had a providential escape last night. I didn't want to scare you, so I didn't tell you about this earlier. The previous stationmaster too left this place because of snakes. Before him, two stationmasters have died of snakebite in the quarters. People don't go anywhere near a place where a black mamba is seen. I'm telling you all this as a friend. Please don't let our employers know that I told you this. Apply for a transfer."

Shankar said, "I'll do that, but it will take some time to get a reply. Meanwhile, please do me a favour. I am totally unarmed. Please get me a gun or a revolver as early as you can. And some carbolic acid. Please give me the acid on your way back."

He asked a train porter to stay back. Together, they spent the day closing all the cracks and crevices everywhere. On close scrutiny, it seemed the snake had come through a crack in the western wall of the station room. These were rat holes. It is possible that a snake from outside had entered the rat hole in search of rats. They closed the hole as well as they could. Shankar collected a bottle of carbolic acid from the guard of the down train. He sprayed the acid in the rooms and around the compound. The porter gave him a strong stick. Within a few days the company sent him a gun.

FOUR

Scarcity of water was a regular feature at Shankar's station. Water supplied by the trains was barely enough for drinking and cooking – not much was left for bathing. The well too had dried up. One day, Shankar came to know that there was a lake about three miles from the station where the water was good. Moreover, there were fish in the lake.

One morning, after the train had left, Shankar walked down to the lake, eager to get into the cool water and also to catch some fish. He had got his fishing rod and lines brought from Mombassa.

Shankar had a Somali porter show him the way. The lake was not very large and had pencil cedars and tall grass all around. After bathing, Shankar sat down with his fishing rod.

Within two hours, he caught a number of small fish which looked like catfish. He wanted to continue fishing for some more time, but knew he could not delay any longer, as he had to reach the station in time for the afternoon train.

He began going to the lake quite often. Sometimes he had a porter for company, but most days, he was alone. The problem of bathing had also been solved.

Gradually, the summer became oppressive. The terrible summer of Africa. It was difficult to go out in the sun after nine in the morning. After eleven, the savannah seemed to have caught fire. But Shankar's colleagues from the trains told him this was nothing compared to the summer in Central and South Africa.

Soon, an incident took place that changed the course of Shankar's life. One afternoon, around three o'clock, while coming back from a fishing trip, he heard someone groaning somewhere in the scorched grassland about a mile away from the station. Shankar figured out the direction the sound came from and went after it. Soon, he saw a man sitting in the sparse shadow of a pencil cedar.

He rushed towards the man. He was a European and was wearing a worn-out jacket and trousers with many patches. He had large eyes, a red beard and a handsome face. It seemed he had a strong physique once, but presently he was abnormally thin, possibly due to disease and starvation. The man, leaning on the tree, was only semi-conscious. A faded Stetson hung on one side of his head and a khaki canvas bag lay by his side.

Shankar asked him in English, "Where are you from?"

Without replying, the man made a sign with his hand to indicate he was thirsty and said, "Water, a little water."

Shankar said, "I have no water with me. Do you think you can lean on me and walk up to the station?"

With great difficulty, the man walked for some distance leaning on Shankar. Towards the end, Shankar carried him on his shoulders. That delayed him. The afternoon train had come and left in his absence. Shankar made a bed for the stranger in the station room and gave him some water and food. He was slightly better by then, but had high fever. His illness was possibly due to extreme fatigue and starvation. Shankar felt he was not likely to recover in a day or two.

The man introduced himself after some time. He was Diego Alvarez – a Portuguese, tanned permanently by the African sun.

At night, he slept in the station room. Shankar did not know

what to do with the sick man. There was no doctor or medicine available. The morning train did not go towards Mombassa. He could be sent to Mombassa with the guard of the afternoon train. But that was a long way off. If only they had been able to come back in time for the afternoon train, there would not have been any trouble at all.

Shankar did not sleep that night. He sat beside the patient, who was just a bag of bones. In this wilderness, far away from home, this sick man had no one to look after him. Only Shankar could do something to help him.

Since childhood, Shankar could not bear to see the suffering of others. Even a close relative could not have nursed the sick man the way Shankar did, with utmost care, through the night.

When the moon rose above the low hills in the east and the stillness of the night filled the vast plain, fierce roars of lions were heard from the savannah. The sick man was in a slumber but on hearing the roar, he got up with a start. Shankar said, "Don't be afraid. The lions are far away and the door is closed."

Shankar went out and stood on the platform. The amazingly beautiful night cast a spell upon him. The moon was close to the distant horizon and the long shadows of the cedars were stretched from east to west. The grassland was quiet, absolutely still. The lion roared again from within five hundred yards behind the station quarters. But Shankar, quite used to these roars by now, was no longer intimidated. Fascinated by the beautiful night, he forgot about the lions.

After some time, the clock struck two and he returned to the room. The man was sitting on his makeshift bed. He said, "Please give me some water."

He spoke fluent English. Shankar poured him some water from the canteen.

By that time his temperature had gone down. He said, "What did you say? You thought I was afraid? Diego Alvarez afraid? Young man, you don't know Diego Alvarez."

A faint smile played upon his lips, a smile that conveyed dejection, despair and sarcasm at the same time. Exhausted, he once again sank back on the bed. Shankar observed the man's smile and felt he was not just a regular, ordinary person. Shankar's eyes chanced upon his fingers which were short and strong. The veins showed on his arms like threads, he had strong jaws underneath the red beard. Everything about him indicated a strong character. With the fever gone, the real man seemed to be emerging slowly.

He said, "Come close to me. You have done me a great favour. If I had a son, he could not have done more. But let me tell you this, I am not going to live. I know my days are numbered. I want to return your favour. Are you an Indian? How much do you earn? If for this pittance you have left your country and come so far, then you must be a brave fellow. And tough. Listen to me carefully, but promise me that before my death, you will not reveal to anybody what I'm going to tell you now."

Shankar gave the man his word. Then, as that amazing night passed slowly, he heard an unbelievably fascinating story, the likes of which are found only in works of fiction.

How old are you, young man? Twenty two? Twenty two years ago, in 1888 or 89, when you were still a baby in your mother's arms, I prospected for gold in a mountain to the north of Cape Colony. At that time, I was young myself and didn't care a fig for the word Danger.

I purchased my provisions in the town of Bulawayo and started off alone, with only two donkeys to carry the luggage. I crossed the Zambezi river, knowing nothing about the place or the country. There were small hills, grasslands and a few villages. Eventually, signs of human habitation ceased. I reached a place where no European had ever set foot before.

Whenever I come across a river or stream, I look for traces of gold. I had read that many fortune hunters had discovered something or the other in South Africa, and had become enormously rich. I had heard so many of these stories since my childhood. In fact it was the lure of these stories that had brought me to Africa. But for two years I wandered about without success. I went through much hardship during that time. Once I even stumbled upon a fortune, but lost it.

One morning, I shot an antelope. I pitched my tent, roasted the meat and had lunch. After that, I went to sleep as it was too hot to walk in the afternoon – the temperature ranged between 115 and 130 degrees Fahreinheit in summers. I had got up and was cleaning my rifle, when I found the gunsight was missing. It is difficult to aim properly without the sight. I searched for it for quite some time, but couldn't find it. There was a mound nearby, on which I saw some small, white, hard stuff. This thing was there in many places on the surface of the mound. I selected one piece, shaped it and fixed it on the barrel of my rifle for the time being. Then in the evening I left the place and moved northwards. Slowly, I forgot where I had camped that morning.

About fifteen days later, I met Jim Carter, an Englishman. Like me, he too was wandering about in search of gold. He had two Matabele porters with him. He too was a vagabond but was older than me. We were pleased to meet each other.

One day, Jim was checking my rifle. Suddenly he said in a surprised voice, "How come you have such an unusual sight?" When I explained the reason, he became excited and said, "Didn't you realize that this thing is pure silver? It is the mineral form of silver. This mineral is usually found in or around a silver deposit. My estimate is that from about a tonne of this stone, we would get at least nine thousand ounces of silver. Let's go there immediately. We will be millionaires soon."

Let me be brief. Along with Carter, I went back the way I had come. But despite our best efforts for four months, despite suffering terribly, despite losing our way in the cruel, flat, desert-like veldt, despite having several close encounters with death, I just couldn't find that place. When I had taken down my tent, I hadn't observed the area carefully. In the African veldt, you don't have any landmarks. Each place looks just like any other. It is difficult to identify a precise location. After many fruitless attempts, we gave up the hope of ever finding the silver mine and started walking towards the River Gwai. Jim Carter did not leave me ... he was with me till his death. It's frightful even to think of his terrible end.

During that expedition, we went through extreme physical hardship, but the worst hardship was thirst. So, we decided to travel only along rivers. Food was not a problem, we used to get plenty of game. When we came across villages, we purchased things like sweet potato and chicken.

Once, we crossed the Orange River and took shelter in a village about fifty miles from the river. There, a daughter of the village chief suddenly fell ill. We saw a small naked girl of five or six violently thrashing about in pain. She had a bad stomachache. All the villagers were crying and running around, convinced that the girl was under the spell of an evil spirit. They were also sure that the spirit would be satisfied only after killing the poor child. After asking her parents, we gathered that she had gone to the jungle and the spirit had entered her body there. I guessed she would have eaten too much of some wild fruit and it was those fruits which were causing all the trouble. I asked her whether she had eaten any fruit in the jungle. Yes, she had. Were the fruits unripe? No, not the fruit. She had eaten the seeds. The seeds were the edible part of that fruit.

The visiting spirit left after a dose of homeopathic medicine from a box of medicines we used to carry. We became honoured guests of the village. We stayed there as the chief's guest for fifteen days. We used to shoot large eland antelope and invite the villagers for dinner. When we were leaving the village, the chief said, "You people love white stones, don't you? They are nice to play with. Would you like to take some? Wait, I'll show you."

In a short while he came back with a stone as big as a fig. Jim and I were stunned. A diamond! An uncut diamond collected from the surface of a diamond reserve or mine.

The chief said, "Please keep this. Can you see that high mountain far away? The one which looks hazy from here? You can reach that mountain within a moon. We have heard that plenty of these stones are found there, although we have never been to the place. It's a dangerous place, the domain of the demigod Bunip. Many moons ago, three daredevil men from our village went there ignoring all warnings. They never came back. On another occasion, a white man like you had come. This was many, many moons ago, in the time of my father or grandfather. He too went there but did not return."

We checked our maps immediately after leaving the village. The hazy mountains far away were the Richtersveldts, the largest, most impenetrable, unknown and dangerous area in southern Africa. Except for a few brave explorers and geologists, no civilized man had ever been there. Most of the regions of this thickly covered mountain were unknown. There was no map, and nobody knew anything about the place.

Both Jim and I could feel the blood racing in our veins. We were convinced that the mountain and the forest were awaiting us with their enormous secret treasure. We had to go there.

Seventeen days after leaving the village, we reached the dense forest at the foothills of the Richtersveldt Mountains.

I have already told you that this mountain is in one of the most difficult terrains in South Africa. We did not find human habitation near the place. The forest seemed impenetrable, it was as if no woodcutter had ever entered that jungle.

We had reached the place a little before sunset. As per Jim's suggestion, we pitched our camp there for the night. Jim gathered dry twigs from the forest for lighting a fire and I started cooking. We had shot two wildfowl in the morning. I was planning to roast them. I was busy plucking the feathers off the birds, when Jim said, "Leave the birds. Let's have some coffee first."

The fire was roaring. I put the kettle on and started working on the birds again when we heard a lion roaring from close quarters. As Jim left with his rifle, I told him, "It's getting dark, don't go too far."

I was still skinning the birds, when I heard two gunshots. After a few seconds, there was another shot. Then it was all quiet. Ten minutes passed. Seeing no sign of Jim, I took my rifle and went out towards the direction of the sound. I saw Jim coming, pulling something heavy behind him. He said, "An excellent hide. It'll be finished by hyenas if left outside. Let's drag it to the tent."

We dragged the huge lion close to the campfire. Soon it became dark. We had our supper and went to bed.

Late that night, we were awakened by the roars of a lion. It was roaring nearby. In the darkness I couldn't make out exactly how far it was. I sat up on the bed with my rifle. Jim said, "Must be the mate of the one I killed," turned around and fell asleep immediately. I went out and found the fire had died out. Some dry sticks were still left. I lit the fire again and went back to bed.

Next morning we entered the forest. After some time we met a few natives. They were hunting antelopes in that forest. We requested them to work as our porters and guides and promised to pay them with tobacco.

They said, "You have no idea about this place. If you did, you wouldn't have made such an offer. No one goes deep into this forest. The hill in front of us is low. Once you cross it, you will reach a valley with a dense forest. Beyond the valley is another hill, which is much higher. The valley is a dangerous place. Bunip lives there. No one ever returns from Bunip's territory. Nobody goes there. You expect us to walk into the jaws of death for a little tobacco? You too ought to give up such crazy ideas."

We asked, "What is a Bunip?"

They didn't know. But they made it clear that although they didn't know what Bunip was, they knew too well how much damage it could cause.

Neither of us knew the meaning of the word Fear. Particularly Jim. He insisted that we should unravel the mystery of Bunip – whether we discovered diamonds or not. If only I had understood that it was his death beckoning him ...

The elderly man was tired after talking so long. Shankar was spellbound. He hadn't heard anything like this before. He looked at the torn clothes of the dying man, his stout arms crisscrossed with veins, his joined, grey eyebrows, his blue, steely eyes – and felt great respect and regard for Diego Alvarez.

A real man!

Alvarez said, "Another glass of water."

After drinking the water, he picked up the threads of his story.

... Yes, listen. We continued our journey through the forest. So many large trees, huge ferns, so many colourful orchids and lianas. In some places, the bushes beneath the trees were so thick that we could hardly move forward. The undergrowth was particularly heavy and some of them had sharp thorns. The foliage was so dense that we wondered whether sunlight ever entered that jungle. The sky couldn't be seen. The jungle was home to a large number of baboons of all sizes, and they were a menace. Not scared of humans, they gnashed their teeth at us. Some of the male baboons were very aggressive. They would have attacked us if we didn't have guns. Jim said, "At least, there would be no shortage of food in this jungle."

We walked for seven or eight days. Jim was right. Everyday we killed a baboon for food. Many streams cascaded down the mountain, so there was no shortage of water either. But drinking water from the streams had its own problems. One day, we stopped next to a stream and lit a fire for roasting baboon meat. As Jim was thirsty, he drank plenty of water from the stream. In a short while, he had violent cramps in his stomach and started vomiting. I know a little bit of science. On testing the water, I found it contained a high level of arsenic. Possibly, upstream, the water flowed over a layer of arsenic. I gave Jim a homeopathic medicine from my medicine box. By evening he was better.

In that forest, we didn't come across any animal other than the baboons and a few poisonous snakes. Of course, I'm not counting the birds or the butterflies. Such a variety of birds and butterflies can be seen only in tropical rainforests.

First, we came across a relatively lower range of the Richtersveldt Mountains. After crossing that, we camped in a dense forest in a valley. A narrow stream flowed through the valley. We were happy to find the stream, because rich minerals are often found in or around such streams. We started testing soil samples from the riverbed and nearby areas, but found nothing valuable. There was not a speck of gold. Almost twenty days passed. We began to lose hope. One evening, while we were drinking coffee, Jim said, "I have a feeling we will find gold here. Let's stay put for some more time."

Another twenty days passed. Baboon meat became unbearable and disgusting. Even a person like Jim seemed to be giving up. I said, "Enough is enough, Jim. Let's go back. The tribal chief has played a trick on us. There is no fortune to be found here."

Jim said, "This mountain has many parallel ranges. I will not leave without checking all of them."

One day, while sieving sand from the riverbed, Jim and I

Our faces lit up with surprise and happiness. Jim said, "Diego, at last, the reward for all the hard work! You understand what this is, don't you?

I did. It was a piece of the famous yellow diamond of South Africa. But there was no cause for cheer. There was no deposit near our camp. The stone had been carried downstream by water. It only indicated that in that vast, impregnable forest, there was a reserve of yellow diamonds somewhere. The stream had brought down one piece. It would be a formidable task to locate the deposit proper.

We were prepared to accept the challenge, but the demon that protected that enormous fortune of diamonds interfered abruptly.

One afternoon, we were resting on a patch of clear ground. There was a palm tree closeby. Around the foot of the tree, there were thick shrubs. Suddenly, we saw something was shaking the palm tree vigorously. The leaves of the tree fluttered as if a storm blew through them. The tree trunk was also shaking.

We were baffled. There wasn't any wind blowing, then why was the palm tree shaking so? Jim immediately entered the shrubs to check what was wrong.

Seconds later, there was a cry of excruciating pain from within the shrubs. I rushed in with my rifle and found Jim, badly mauled and bleeding. An exceedingly strong animal had slashed his chest open with sharp nails – it was as if a pillow had been ripped open.

Jim only said, "A demon, a real demon."

He gestured to me … Run … run …

He died within minutes. I went to check the palm tree. A few huge scales were sticking to the tree. It seemed an enormously strong animal had been rubbing itself against the tree, and that was what had made the tree shake so violently. There was no sign of the animal. I pulled Jim's body out of the shrubs into the open area and with my rifle, went to check the other side of the shrubs. I saw the footprints of an animal that had only three toes. I followed the footprints for some distance. The trail ended in front of a cave. At the entrance to the cave, I clearly saw the large footprints with three toes on the dry sand.

By then it had become almost dark. In that desolate, unknown, mountain-ringed valley, I was following a still more unknown and dangerous animal. I looked to my right and saw in the dim evening light a steep basalt wall rising almost four thousand feet high. Very high up, beyond the bamboo groves at the top of the mountains, there was a trace of the last rays of the sun – or perhaps it was a trick played by my eyes. It must have been the glow of the endless sky.

I thought it would not be wise to either enter the cave or to stand outside it as it was dangerous even at the entrance. I returned to the tent and kept vigil over Jim's body through the night, next to a roaring fire, my rifle by my side.

Next morning, I buried Jim and started looking for the animal again. But the problem was that in spite of a thorough search, I couldn't find that cave. There were many such caves in that mountain. I didn't know which one I had seen in the fading light of the previous evening.

It was not possible to continue in that dangerous forest alone. I walked for fifteen days and reached the village. They received me well. I told them how Jim had died.

They were visibly scared. Their small eyes bulged. They said, "Oh god! Bunip. That's why no one goes into that forest."

I walked for another five days from the village to the Orange River. There I caught a Dutch boat and returned to civilization.

I could not explore the Richtersveldts again, although I tried to, many times. In between, there was the Boer War. I went to the battlefield. I was injured and spent a long time in a hospital in Pretoria. After recovery, I got a job in an orange orchard and lived there until recently.

After living a quiet life for four or five years, I was tired of it. So I came out again. But I am old now, I think my journey is coming to an end ... Please keep this map. It gives a rough direction of the Richtersveldt Mountain and the river where we found the diamond. If you have courage, go there. You will be a rich man. After the Boer War, two or three diamond deposits were discovered near the Wai River in that area. But no one knows the place where we found the diamond. You should go there...

Diego Alvarez completed his story. Exhausted, he lay back on the bed again.

FIVE

Thanks to Shankar's nursing, Alvarez recovered quickly. He stayed with Shankar for two weeks. But a born wanderer like him could not remain in the same place for long. Soon, he became restless and one day, he decided to leave.

In the meantime, Shankar too had made up his mind. He asked Alvarez, "Do you remember what you told me when you were sick? About the diamond reserve?"

The elderly man had shared his secrets during his illness, but now did not broach the subject again. He was quiet throughout the day. Then in the evening he said, "It's not that I haven't thought it over. But do you have the courage to go after a chimera?"

Shankar said, "Let's test if I do. If you agree, I'll send a telegram to the Tsavo station calling for a replacement today itself."

Alvarez thought for a while and then said, "Send it then. But know this first. Those who prospect for gold or diamond, don't always find them. I knew an eighty year old man who had never found anything. But he always said, Now I have the correct information. Soon I'll strike it rich. He prospected in the Australian deserts and the African veldt till his death."

Ten days later, Alvarez and Shankar left for Kisumu. From there, they would board a steamer on Lake Victoria and sail to Mwanza in the south.

On the way to Kisumu, they came across a grassland where thousands of giraffes, zebras and gazelles were grazing. Shankar was dumbfounded. He had never seen anything like this. The giraffes were not afraid of people. They moved away by about fifty yards and watched the two men with curiosity.

Alvarez said, "One needs a special license from the African government for shooting giraffe. Not everyone can do so. That's the reason they're so bold."

But the gazelles were very timid. In a herd, there were two or three hundred of them. One of them looked up while grazing and the next moment the entire herd galloped away to the other end of the valley.

The steamer left the small port of Kisumu. It was a British vessel. As Shankar and Alvarez did not have much money, they were travelling on the deck. African women boarded the ship carrying chickens in their hands and babies on their backs. Masai workers were going home on leave, carrying glass beads, inexpensive trinkets and mirrors purchased from Nairobi.

Alvarez and Shankar got off the steamer at Mwanza and started off on foot. They would trek three hundred miles to Tabora. After resting for a few days there, they would go to Port Ujiji on the edge of Tanganyika Lake.

On the way, Alvarez said to Shankar, "It is most unsafe to walk through Tanganyika. There is a kind of fly here that causes sleeping sickness. Almost the entire population of Tanganyika has been wiped out by this epidemic. Besides, the area between Mwanza and Tabora is also infested with lions. In fact, you can call this area the Lion Country."

Ten miles from the town, they came across a small thatched bungalow. A European hunter was staying there. He was very friendly towards Alvarez, but on seeing Shankar he asked Alvarez, "This boy seems to be an Indian – where did you find him? Is he your porter?"

Alvarez replied, "He is my son."

The man raised his eyebrows. Alvarez then described in detail his illness and what Shankar had done for him. But he did not give the slightest hint about their destination or the purpose of their journey.

The man smiled and said, "That's nice. Your boy seems to be both brave and kind. I have heard that the Hindus of East Indies are good people. Once, in Uganda, a Sikh was very nice to me, I'll never forget his hospitality. Tonight, you are welcome to stay as my guests. This is a government bungalow. Like you, I have been trekking throughout the day. I came here only this afternoon."

The gentleman had a portable gramophone. In the evening, after finishing their dinner of tinned tomatoes and sardines, they sat outside the bungalow and listened to music. A lion roared nearby. It was probably roaring with its head close to the ground, because the earth reverberated with the roar. The gentleman said, "Tanganyika is the land of lions and they are extremely ferocious. Most of them have tasted human blood and seem to have developed a liking for it."

Shankar pondered over this piece of cheerful news. From his experience at the railway camp in Uganda, he knew only too well how dangerous they could be.

The next morning, they started off again. The hunter cautioned them about the sleeping sickness flies which were usually seen after sunrise. They could not be allowed to bite.

Alvarez and Shankar were following a narrow trail through a field of tall grass. Alvarez said, "Be careful. Lions often hide behind tall grass. Don't fall behind."

For Shankar, the only comfort was that Alvarez was

carrying a gun and he was, what you may call, a Crack-shot. But even then, Shankar did not feel too secure. He knew that lions were capable of picking up their victims quietly, all of a sudden. There would be no time to even take the rifle off your back.

About an hour before sunset that day, they made camp for the night in a wide open field. Alvarez said, "There's no village nearby. It wouldn't be safe to walk after dark."

They put up a small tent by hanging two pieces of canvas under a massive baobab tree. Shankar lit a fire with dry leaves and twigs and started cooking. Tired after the long walk, they fell asleep in no time.

Late in the night Shankar woke up with a start when Alvarez called him. Alvarez said, under his breath, "There is an animal close to our tent. Pick up your gun."

They could hear a large animal breathing through the thin canvas of the tent. In the dim light of the fading campfire, the baobab looked like a terrible demon. Shankar was about to get out of the bed with his gun, but the old man stopped him.

The next moment, the animal tried to rush into their tent. Alvarez fired two shots. Shankar too raised his gun and took aim. But before he could press the trigger, Alvarez's rifle boomed once again.

Then it was all quiet.

They switched on their torch and came out carefully. The torchlight showed a huge lion that had tried to enter the tent. It was still alive, but badly injured. It breathed its last after they fired two more shots.

Alvarez looked at the stars and said, "The night is still young. Let's catch up on our sleep."

They went in and lay down. In a short while, Shankar was surprised to hear his companion snoring. He, however, could not go back to sleep.

After half an hour, all the lions in the savannah seemed to compete with Alvarez's snoring. They roared in unison. How frightening that roaring was. Shankar was familiar with the lion's roar, but this was different. He never forgot that horrifying roar in his life. Plus, it could not have been more than ten yards from the tent.

Alvarez woke up and said, "Damn! It's not going to let us sleep. Must be the mate of the dead one. Be careful. They are dangerous in these situations."

It was an awful experience. The fire had almost died out. There was complete darkness outside. A thin canvas separated them from a desperate animal that had just lost its mate. It continued to roar. At times, it came close and at times, went a little away. And at others, it circled the tent.

The lion left a little before dawn. They too struck camp and started off.

SIX

About fifteen days later, Shankar and Alvarez boarded a steamer at the port of Ujiji on Lake Tanganyika. After crossing the lake, they purchased a few essential things at a small town called Albertville. Between Albertville and Kabalo, there was a rail line run by the Belgian government. From Kabalo they would sail again for three days, this time on the Congo River, towards Sunkini. At Sunkini, they would leave the river behind and go southwards, into unmapped forests and deserts.

A dingy town, Kabalo was a den of shady characters, mostly crossbred people of Portuguese and Belgian origins. As Shankar stepped out of the railway station, a Portuguese accosted him, "Hello! Where are you off to? You seem to be new here! I'm sure you don't know me. I am Albuquerque!"

Shankar looked behind. Alvarez was yet to come out of the station.

The man was ugly and crude. But he was a giant of a man, about seven feet tall. He was so well-built that every muscle in his body stood out.

Shankar said stiffly, "Pleased to meet you."

The man said, "So, black fellow, you are from East Indies, aren't you? Come, play a hand of poker with me."

Shankar was angry. He said, "I am not interested in playing poker with you." He knew that poker was only a pretext. The man wanted to cheat him of his possessions. Shankar had heard that poker was a kind of gambling with cards. He had no idea how it was played but he had heard that in Nairobi, crooks cheated tourists by playing poker with them. This was a kind of robbery.

The Portuguese rogue flared up on hearing Shankar's reply. He frowned, came closer, gnashed his teeth and said in a contorted voice, "What did you say, you wretched nigger? You seem to be too smart for an Indian. For your benefit, let me tell you that Albuquerque's pistol has done away with scores of dirty niggers like you. Listen to me carefully, my rules are simple. Whenever a new fellow arrives at Kabalo, he has to either play poker with me or face me in a gun duel."

Shankar knew that a duel with this rogue would mean instant death. Albuquerque was a thug, possibly a crack-shot, Shankar had no chance against him in a gun duel. After all, till the other day, he had been a railway clerk. On the other hand, if he chose to play poker, he would lose all his money.

Perhaps Shankar took half a minute to ponder over this. The man removed his pistol from the holster in a flash, held it

on Shankar's stomach and said, "Duel or poker?"

The crude challenge made Shankar's blood boil. He would not submit to brute force, even if it meant death. He was about to say Duel, when someone behind them said in a very loud voice, "Careful! Or I'm going to blow your brains off."

Both of them started and turned towards the voice. Alvarez stood firmly, his Winchester repeater aimed at Albuquerque's head. Shankar took advantage of the situation and slipped behind Albuquerque's pistol. Alvarez said, "So, you want a duel with a boy? Shame on you. Drop your gun before I count three. One ... two ..."

The pistol dropped from Albuquerque's hand.

Alvarez said, "Playing the bully with a boy?"

Shankar was quick to pick up Albuquerque's pistol. Albuquerque was puzzled. He had not expected someone like Alvarez to come to Shankar's rescue. He smiled and said, "All right, mate, I'm sorry, you win. Young lad, return my pistol. Don't be afraid, you too are a mate. Let's shake hands. Albuquerque doesn't bear a grudge. My cabin is just round the corner, come and join me for a glass of beer."

Alvarez knew his own people well. He accepted the invitation and went to Albuquerque's cabin. Since Shankar did not drink beer, Albuquerque made coffee for him. He talked to them as if nothing had happened, shared jokes and laughed heartily.

He made a deep and lasting impression on Shankar. Albuquerque had completely forgotten the insult and defeat and talked to them as if they were long lost friends. Indeed, he belonged to a rare breed of men.

The next day, they boarded a steamer at Kabalo and sailed

southwards. Shankar was thrilled to watch the scenery on the banks of the river. He had not seen such lush green forests earlier. Until now, he had been in parts of Africa that did not have dense forests. He had seen the savannah, which was mostly bare grasslands but for some trees like cedars and acacias. But here, as the steamer moved southwards, the jungles on the banks became more variegated. There were massive trees with thick foliage, thick, large creepers and countless varieties of flowers. Shankar felt Mother Nature was beside herself with joy, as though she was enjoying her own beauty and abundance.

Shankar was not a hardened prospector like Diego Alvarez. He had grown up in the green fields of Bengal. The artist in him was lost in the profusion of beauty of the golden afternoons, and wove it into the warp and weft of his imagination.

At night Shankar saw the mysterious flora and fauna coming to life under a foreign sky shining with stars. He heard the cries of wild animals from the jungle. Lost in the dark splendour, he stayed awake, ignoring the cold of the Central African night.

There, the brightly shining constellation of the Ursa Major. Thousands of miles away, the same constellation must have risen over his small village tonight. And the slender new moon must be shining over his village too. He had come a long way from that familiar sky. No one knew how much further he would travel, and what would be the outcome!

Two days later, the boat reached Sunkini. From there, they started trekking again. The area they covered did not have a forest ... it was an immense, desolate plain with countless big and small hills. Most of them were barren, but for a few shrubs like euphorbia. Shankar liked the place. There was a sense of freedom in such vast open spaces. The colours of twilight and the magic of moonlight transformed the afternoons and nights of Africa into a fairy tale kingdom.

Alvarez, however, said, "This veldt looks the same everywhere, you could easily lose your way here."

A mishap occurred that very day. After sunset, they pitched camp by the side of a hillock and lit a fire. Shankar went out in search of water. He carried Alvarez's rifle, but took only two cartridges. About half an hour passed, a thin veil of darkness covered the veldt slowly. Suddenly, looking around him, Shankar felt uncomfortable and sensed an impending danger. He decided to return to the camp immediately.

The horizon was dotted with craggy hills on all sides, but there was no landmark! The landscape looked identical in all directions. Shankar continued to walk but within a few minutes realized that he had lost his way. He recalled Alvarez's words of caution. But because of his lack of experience, he did not realize how grave the situation was. He kept on walking. At times he felt the camp was ahead of him, at times to his left, then to his right. Why couldn't he see the campfire? Where was the small hillock?

Shankar panicked after walking for two hours. He accepted the fact that he had no clue about the way back to their camp. He was in serious trouble. Alone in this lion infested veldt of Rhodesia, he would have to face a severely cold night without a blanket. He did not even have a matchbox to light a fire. He had nothing to eat or drink.

To cut a long story short, the next evening, that is, almost twenty four hours later, Alvarez rescued a dazed, exhausted, thirsty and almost dying Shankar from under an euphorbia tree seven miles from their camp.

Alvarez said, "If I didn't find you, you would have continued to walk, and would have gone deeper into the desert and possibly died of thirst by tomorrow afternoon. Many people have lost their lives this way in the Rhodesian veldt. This is a dangerous place. Don't ever leave the camp alone as you are completely inexperienced. You will definitely die."

Shankar said, "Alvarez, you have saved my life twice. I'll never forget this."

Alvarez said, "Don't forget, young man, you did me the same favour earlier. If you were not there, by now my bones would have been bleached white by the sun in the grasslands of Uganda."

It took them two months to cross the veldt between Rhodesia and Angola. At last, far away, a cloudlike mountain range became visible. Alvarez checked his map and said, "That is our destination ... the Richtersveldt Mountains. It is still forty miles away. In these vast open plains of Africa, you can see things from far away."

There were many baobab trees in the area. Shankar really liked these trees. From a distance, they looked like peepal or banyan, but from up close, the short tree offered little shade. It had a thick trunk, crooked branches and large outgrowths on its trunk. It looked like an ugly, short, hunchbacked monster straight out of the pages of *The Arabian Nights*.

They were sitting around a fire on a bitterly cold evening, when Alvarez said, "This Rhodesian veldt has diamonds everywhere ... this is a land of diamonds. You must have heard of the Kimberly mines. There are many more. People have found large and small pieces of diamonds in many places. They can be found even now."

Almost immediately he said, "Who are these people?"

Shankar was facing Alvarez. He turned around but could not see anyone. He asked, "Who are you talking about?"

But Alvarez's keen eyes, like his bullets, missed nothing. After a few minutes, Shankar spotted a few indistinct figures walking towards their camp. Alvarez said, "Shankar, load the revolver and give it to me quickly."

Shankar came out of the tent with the gun and saw Alvarez smoking quietly, without betraying any emotion. Some people were coming towards their camp through the darkness. A little later, they stood in front of the campfire. They were tall, dark, well-built men. They did not carry anything, had nothing on them except loincloths, lion's manes around their necks and feathers in their hair. In the firelight, they looked like bronze statues.

Alvarez asked them in Zulu, "What brings you here?"

He talked to them for sometime after which they sat down. Alvarez said, "Shankar, give them some food."

Then he said under his breath, "Be very careful! We are in grave danger. Be on your guard."

They opened some cans. Shankar served food to the strangers. Alvarez too joined them, although he and Shankar had already had their supper. Shankar guessed that either Alvarez had something on his mind, or it was customary in these parts to dine with one's guests.

Alvarez kept talking to the strangers in Zulu. After some time they finished eating and left. Each of them was given a cigarette before leaving.

After they had left, Alvarez said, "These people are the Matabeles, a fierce tribe. They have fought many wars with the British government. They suspect we are prospecting for diamonds. This place is within the domain of their chief. No civilized government has control over them. They will simply take us with them and burn us at the stake. Let's take down the tent and leave this place right away."

Shankar enquired, "Why did you ask me to get the revolver?"

Alvarez smiled and said, "Oh! It was only a precaution. If they were not satisfied despite our hospitality, or if I sensed they wanted to harm us, I would have shot them. See, I had the revolver behind me when I sat down to eat. I was prepared to finish them. My name is Diego Alvarez. I have never feared the devil. I don't, even now. They would have been dead before they knew what hit them."

After walking another five, six days, they entered a dense tropical rainforest on the foothills of a high mountain. The forest was so vast and gloomy that Shankar felt if he lost his way in here, he would never come out of it alive. Alvarez also cautioned, "Be very careful, Shankar! Unless you know these forests thoroughly, you might lose your way in no time. Many people have died this way. You may get confused about the direction here just as you had been in the desert. Because here too, all the places look alike and there are no landmarks. You have to learn the tricks of the bushmen to survive in these forests. And please don't forget one thing. Always carry your gun. The forests in Central Africa are not recreation parks."

The last statement was hardly necessary. Shankar knew the dangers in these jungles pretty well. He asked, "That yellow diamond mine of yours, how far is it from here? From the map, it seems we are in the Richtersveldt Mountains."

Alvarez said, "You have no idea about the Richtersveldts. We have reached only the outermost range. There are many more. The whole area is enormous. If we walk seventy miles towards the east and hundred and fifty miles towards the west, we would still not come out of the forest. The narrowest width of this forest is forty miles. The total area of this mountain forest is about eight to nine thousand square miles. It would not be easy to find out the exact area where I had come seven, eight years ago. This is not a child's play, young man."

Shankar said, "But we have run out of rations. We'll have to start hunting, or from tomorrow, we'll have to survive on air."

Alvarez said, "Don't worry. Can't you see the hordes of baboons on the trees all around us? If nothing else is available, we can treat ourselves to baboon meat and coffee. But that's for tomorrow. Let's put up the tent and take rest."

They pitched tent under a tall tree and lit a fire. Shankar cooked. They finished their meal and sat in front of the fire. There was still some time to sunset.

Alvarez put the usual strong tobacco in his pipe and started smoking. He said, "Did you know Shankar, in these remote forests of Africa, there are many animals still unknown to scientists? Very few civilized people have explored these forests. A mammal called okapi was first seen in 1900. There is a species of wild boar three times the size of normal wild boars. In 1888, an explorer and a famous hunter, Moses Crowley, first came across the species in the Lualaba jungle of Belgian Congo. With great difficulty, he managed to shoot one of them and presented the specimen to the New York Zoological

Museum. Have you heard of the famous Rhodesian Monster?"

"No, what is it?"

"I'll tell you. There is a large marsh to the north of Rhodesia. Many Zulu tribesmen have seen an extra-ordinary animal in  that marsh. They say the animal's head is like a crocodile's, but it has a horn like the rhino. It has a long neck like the python, but has scales. It has a body like a hippo, but the tail again is like a crocodile. It is a huge animal and is believed to be exceedingly ferocious. No one has seen the animal outside water. But it is difficult to believe the descriptions given by these uncivilized locals.

"But in 1880, a prospector, James Martin, had travelled extensively in that area in search of gold. Mr Martin was the aide-de-camp of General Mathew. He was also a good geologist and zoologist. He has mentioned in his diary that he saw the Rhodesian Monster from a distance. He has written that the animal looked like the pre-historic dinosaurs and was enormous in size. But he was not very sure about the details as he had seen it from far away through dense early morning fog in the marshlands near the Kovirando Lake. The animal made a sound like the neigh of a horse. That was sufficient to send his Zulu porters scurrying for safety. As they ran away, they screamed, Sahab, run, run. Dingonek, dingonek. Dingonek is the animal's Zulu name. The animal is rarely seen, at the most once in two or three years, but it is so destructive that the local people panic whenever it is seen. Mr Martin wrote that he had fired twice from his 303 rifle, but most probably missed the animal from such a distance. It dived into the water, possibly because of the sound of the gunshot."

Shankar asked him, "How did you get these details? Has the diary been published?"

"No. Many years ago, the incident was published in the *Bulawayo Chronicle*. At that time, I had just come to Africa. I was also prospecting in Rhodesia and naturally, I got interested in the story. I kept the newspaper clipping for quite some time. Then somehow, it got lost. It was the newspaper which had christened the animal as the Rhodesian Monster."

Shankar said, "Have you ever come across any strange, unknown animals?"

An extraordinary thing happened as soon as Shankar asked this question. By then, darkness had descended upon the forest. In that fading light, Shankar saw, he might have been wrong but Shankar thought he saw, the strong, fearless Alvarez, the hardened hunter and prospector Alvarez, start on hearing the question. And, this was the most incredible part – the next moment, he trembled.

Alvarez looked around, as if in a stupor, and observed the cheerless jungle and the mysterious, steep mountain without saying a word. As if he was reliving some horrendous experience he had had in this forest long ago, an experience whose memory was not at all pleasant.

Alvarez was afraid!

This was unbelievable. Shankar never thought Alvarez could be frightened by anything. But Alvarez was indeed afraid! And his fear cast its shadow over Shankar too. It was as if this unknown, mysterious forest, protected by an invincible wall of a steep mountain, had been hiding some secret for ages. It threw a challenge to the brave and the fearless, "Come forward to unravel my mystery, but be prepared to sacrifice your life."

The Richtersveldt Mountain is not like the Himalayas, the lord of all mountains and the abode of gods. Like some of the tribes of this continent, its soul too is cruel, barbaric, hungry for human flesh.

SEVEN

Two days passed. They were slowly going deeper inside the forest. Their path was never even, it kept rising and falling. There were small areas covered by tall and rough tussock grass. Water was scarce. In between, even if they came across a few streams, Alvarez would not let Shankar touch that water. It was not easy for a thirsty man to refrain from drinking the crystal clear water of the mountain streams. But Alvarez insisted Shankar drink cold tea instead. Cold tea hardly quenches thirst like water. Indeed, of all the hardship they faced, the worst was the shortage of drinking water.

One day, they had camped in a place where the tussock was very thick. Moreover, it was covered by a thick fog. A little late in the morning, the fog cleared for some time. Looking ahead, Shankar found a steep, imposing ascent blocking their way.

Shankar could not make out how high the ascent was because its top was hidden behind clouds.

"The main range of the Richtersveldt," Alvarez said.

Shankar asked him, "Isn't there any other way? Do we have to cross this?"

Alvarez said, "Yes, because the last time Jim and I had approached the mountain from the south. We reached the foothills of the main range, but we didn't cross it. The stream where we found the yellow diamond flows from east to west. Now we are going from north to south. Therefore, to reach the stream, we have to necessarily cross this range."

Shankar said, "The fog is too thick. I feel it would be better if we started a little later."

They pegged their tent and had their food. Till midday, the fog did not clear. Shankar fell asleep in the tent. When he woke up, it was almost dark. He came out of the tent rubbing his eyes and found Alvarez studying the map with a worried face.

"Shankar, he said, we have a long way to go. Look there, in front of you."

Shankar looked up. What he saw was awesome. The fog had cleared. The main range of the enormous Richtersveldt Mountain rose before them, right up to the sky. The waist of the mountain was covered by thick thunderclouds. But the peak of the mountain, gorgeously lit up by the setting sun, stood like the golden pinnacle of a heavenly temple against the backdrop of a deep blue sky.

It would be impossible to climb the incline they faced – only steep ascent all the way, offering hardly any foothold. Alvarez said, "We can't climb the mountain from here. I'm sure you would agree, from what you can see. Let's go westwards. We'll go around the mountain till we find a pass low enough. We'll cross there. But, in this hundred and fifty mile long range, it may take us more than a month to find a suitable pass."

However, after walking for only five or six days towards the west, they came across a place where the mountain slope was relatively less steep. They decided to climb from there.

Next morning when they started climbing, Shankar's watch showed six thirty. By nine, he felt tired. The altitude increased by six thousand feet within four miles, so one can imagine how exceedingly difficult it was to climb the slope. Besides, the higher they climbed, the denser the jungle became and it was nearly dark all around. By this time, the sun should be high up in the sky, but no sunlight pierced that thick jungle. They could not even see the sky.

There was no trail. They faced an endless array of hoary old thick trunks rising along the mountain slope, reaching for the sky. The jungle floor was wet and slippery, and the rocks were covered with moss, but Shankar could not make out where the water came from. If they slipped, they would fall hundreds of feet below and hurt themselves against sharp rocks.

Neither Shankar nor Alvarez talked. Exhausted by the steep climb, they were breathing heavily. Shankar was more tired. He had been brought up in the plains of Bengal and had no experience of climbing mountains.

Shankar pegged away, hoping Alvarez would soon call it a day. He was unable to climb any more, but was determined to go on till his last breath. He was not prepared to admit to Alvarez that he could climb no more. Alvarez might think the people of East Indies were real weaklings. He was a

representative of Bharotborsho in this inaccessible mountain forest. He couldn't do anything that would let his country down.

It was a lovely forest, a fairytale country! Streams cascaded down the mountain slope and the trees were full of parrots. The birds dazzled Shankar with their magnificent array of colours. There were lovely white flowers on tall grass and orchids hung from branches and tree trunks.

Suddenly, in the trees, Shankar saw some monkeys with long beards, looking like really small, elderly sanyasis. They sat with serious faces, trying to act like real hermits.

Alvarez said, "These are the females of the Colobus species. The males of the species do not have a beard, but the females do – foot long beards and moustaches. And they are very serious, as you can see."

Shankar could not but laugh seeing these funny creatures.

Beneath their feet, there was neither hard soil, nor rock. Instead, there was a soggy layer of rotten leaves and stubs of uprooted trees. Leaves collected in those forests for centuries. They gathered, decayed, and got covered by thick moss and toadstools. On these, dry leaves, broken branches and uprooted trees kept falling. The cycle went on ... At certain places, the layer of decayed leaves was as much as sixty to seventy feet deep.

Alvarez taught Shankar to move with extreme caution on that dangerous terrain. There were places where a man could step in and disappear within the leaves. Just as he might fall into unused wells while walking carelessly in villages. Unless rescued quickly, one was sure to die of suffocation.

The **Bharotborsho** Shankar is referring to is the pre-Partition India which included present day Bangladesh and Pakistan.

Shankar said, "We have to cleave our way through. It's becoming too thick to continue."

The elephant grass, sharp as razor, was like double edged Roman swords. They felt very insecure while moving through this as they could not see beyond a few feet. They knew only too well that danger might strike any moment. Tigers, lions, snakes. It could be anything.

At times, Shankar heard sounds of distant drumbeats. He wondered if there were tribesmen in this forest. He asked Alvarez about the peculiar sound.

Alvarez said, "What you hear is not drums. Some baboons or chimpanzees beat their breast and produce a drum-like sound. There is no question of human beings living in this forest."

Shankar said, "But didn't you say there are no gorillas here?"

"Not gorillas, perhaps. As far as we know, gorillas are found only in some regions of the Belgian Congo, the Ruwenzori Alps and the volcanic mountains of Virunga. But there are other apes which make such a sound by beating their breasts."

After reaching four and a half thousand feet, they stopped for the day and pitched their tent. At night, there were innumerable sounds in this truly tropical rainforest. Shankar was overcome by a sense of amazement. The nocturnal sounds of the rainforest were so diverse and so scary that he could not close his eyes at all. It wasn't only fear. It was fear mixed with awe.

There was an orchestra of sounds. The laughter of hyenas, the screeching noise of the Colobus monkeys, apes beating their breasts and leopards growling – in nature's very own zoo, nobody slept at night. The forest, in the middle of the night, seemed to be possessed by a spirit. Shankar recalled that a few years ago, a circus troop had camped in a field next to their school hostel. The boys in the hostel could not sleep at night due to the cries of the circus animals. But more than any of this, Shankar was really scared when he heard some elephants trumpeting close to their tent. He woke up Alvarez who said, "There's a fire outside our tent. They will not come this way."

Next morning, they started again. Climbing continuously, they passed through a dense jungle of bamboo grass. Underneath were wild ginger plants. On their left, within fifty yards of them, a huge herd of elephants passed by, trampling the green bamboo shoots with a ferocious sound.

At a height of five thousand feet, there was a riot of colours with wild flowers in full bloom. There were bright red erythronia on tall trees. The flowers of the ipomoea creepers reminded Shankar of the bon-kalmi flowers back home, although these flowers were of a lighter shade of violet. The air seemed heavy with the fragrance of white veronicas. Wild coffee plants were in bloom and so were the colourful begonias. It was nature's own garden in the kingdom of clouds ... At times, white clouds gathered around the top of the trees, and then they came down to drench the veronica beds.

At an altitude of seven and a half thousand feet, there was a sudden and drastic change in the landscape. It had taken them two more days to reach that height. It was tough going all the way and Shankar had a terrible pain in his back. The trees at this level were quite different. The trunks and branches were covered with thick moss. Moss was hanging from the branches too, some of them so long that they almost reached the ground. They swung gently when a breeze passed through the forest. There was not much sunlight, as if it was twilight throughout the day. Above all, an eerie silence sat heavily upon the forest.

In that part of the forest, no bird sang, no animal howled, no man ever spoke. The forest was like hell, and the trees stood like ugly, revolting, bearded phantoms guarding that hell.

In the afternoon Alvarez decided to stop for the day. Shankar sat outside their tent drinking coffee and thinking about the forest ... These jungles had not changed since the beginning of life on earth, when the plants were yet to take the shapes that we see today, when enormous reptiles roamed freely in dark forests that covered the earth. Shankar felt he had, by some magic, travelled back in time.

Darkness descended quickly and enveloped the dense forest. They lit a fire outside their tent, but in that absolute darkness, the fire gave but a mere glimmer of light. Nothing was visible beyond the small ring of light. Shankar was surprised by the pindrop silence in that part of the forest. He could not fathom why there was none of the wide medley of night-time sounds they heard elsewhere in the forest. Alvarez was studying the map with furrowed brows. He said, "Shankar, we have climbed eight thousand feet, but we still haven't found the pass through which we expected to cross the range. How much more can we climb? What do we do if the saddle is not in this part?"

The doubt had crossed Shankar's mind too. That day, while climbing, he had looked up through the field glasses a number of times. But throughout the day, the higher ranges had been hidden behind the clouds and he had not been able to see anything. How much higher could they climb? What if they could not find a flat pass to cross over? It would be disastrous if they had to go down from there and start climbing afresh from another point.

He enquired, "What does the map say?"

From the expression on Alvarez's face, it seemed he had lost faith in the map. He replied, "This map doesn't give much details. Who has ever climbed these mountains that a proper map would be made? No one has actually surveyed this area. The map we have was prepared by Sir Philipo De' Philip, who became famous after climbing the Fernando Po peak in Portuguese West Africa. A few years ago, he participated in an expedition led by the great mountaineer and explorer, the Duke of Abruzi. But Sir Philip didn't actually scale the Richtersveldts. I don't think the contours shown in this map are accurate. I can't really understand."

Suddenly, Shankar exclaimed, "What was that?"

First, there was a muffled sound outside their tent. Then they heard someone coughing painfully, as if a terminally ill phthisis patient was coughing desperately in great pain. They heard it once, twice … It stopped. It was obvious to Shankar that the sound was not human.

Immediately, he took his gun and was about to go out of the tent, when Alvarez got up and stopped him hurriedly. Shankar was dumbfounded. He asked, "What was that sound?" He looked at Alvarez and was surprised to see Alvarez looking pale. Was it because of what he had heard just then?

Immediately, they could hear a heavy but fleet-footed animal moving through the jungle beyond the small area lit by the campfire.

No words were exchanged for quite sometime. Then Alvarez said, "Put some more wood into the fire. Check if our rifles are loaded." He was grim, Shankar did not dare ask him any questions.

The night passed without any incident. The next morning, Shankar woke up first. He had to light a fire for making coffee. He went a little away from the tent to pick up dry wood. Suddenly he saw a footprint on the soft ground. It was more than eleven inches in length but had only three toes. The impression of the toes was very clear. He followed the footprints for some time. There were a number of them and each had only three toes!

Shankar remembered Jim Carter's terrible death, as described by Alvarez at the railway station in Uganda. The footprint with three toes on the sand at the entrance of the cave ... He also remembered what the chief of the tribesmen had told them ...

He immediately recalled the pale, frightened face of Alvarez the previous evening. On another occasion too, Alvarez had been similarly frightened, the day on which they camped at the foothills of the mountain.

Bunip! Bunip of the tribal chief's tale. The terror of the Richtersveldt Mountain and forest, who ensures neither people nor animals venture into this forest eight thousand feet above the plains. The reason why they hadn't heard the sound of any animals the previous night struck him in a flash. Even Alvarez was frightened on hearing its voice. Perhaps he was not unfamiliar with it.

That morning, Alvarez got up a little late. After hot coffee and a light breakfast, he was transformed back to the fearless and heroic Alvarez who could challenge anyone, man or demon. Shankar deliberately did not show him the footprints. Who knows, he might decide to go back and start afresh from another point to look for the saddle!

Soon it started raining heavily. Rainwater made thousands of rivulets that danced down the mountain slope. The mountain and forest confused Shankar. They had climbed to such a height, but from any point, when he looked at a thousand feet below, the lower level seemed to be the plains. That created an illusion as if they had climbed only so much.

It continued raining throughout the day. After waiting for some time, at ten o'clock Alvarez decided to start, much to his companion's dismay. Shankar saw no point in getting drenched. He felt nothing much would be lost if they were delayed by a day. That morning, Shankar learnt a lesson as he observed how seriously a white man took his work.

They climbed throughout the day in pouring rain. Shankar was exhausted by that seemingly neverending journey. They were drenched to the bones. All their provisions, tent and clothes were wet too. There was not even a dry handkerchief between the two of them. Shankar felt numb in body and mind. By evening, when the dark mountain forest looked frighteningly sombre under an overcast sky, Shankar wondered why he had undertaken such a long journey through that unknown forest in an alien land inhabited by ferocious animals, towards an uncertain diamond reserve, or more likely, towards death. He hardly knew Alvarez, why did he follow him? He did not need diamonds. His thatched house in Bengal, the tranquil village paths shaded by familiar trees, the placid river, the sweet trills of birds he knew since childhood ... all that now seemed unreal, as though seen in a dream. No diamond reserve of Africa could be more precious than that.

But later in the night, when the moon rose in a cloudless sky, he got over his depression. The ethereal moonlit night was beyond description. Shankar was no longer in the known world, there was no place called Bengal. Everything had melted into a distant dream. He did not want to return anywhere, he did not want diamonds, did not want wealth. Far above the temporal world, he now belonged to a lily-white land of gods. No man has ever seen the beauty that surrounds him. No man has ever listened to such absorbing silence. In the depths of night, the remote, enormous Richtersveldt Mountain and forest, kneeling down to meditate on itself in this kingdom of clouds! Rarely does a mortal man have the good fortune to visit such a world.

He woke up from sleep suddenly as Alvarez called him urgently, "Shankar! Shankar! Get up, pick up the rifle."

"What is it?"

Then he listened carefully. Something was moving around their tent, its laboured breathing could be heard distinctly. There was complete darkness outside as the moon had set. The last rays of moonlight were reflected by the treetops. The fire in front of their tent was still burning weakly, but it was so small that it hardly lit the surrounding area.

There was a loud noise of branches being broken. It seemed as if a heavy animal was fleeing hastily through the jungle. Perhaps it had realized that the people in the tent were awake, and that it would not be able to catch them unawares.

Whatever the animal might be, it was intelligent and alert!

Alvarez went out with an electric torch and a rifle. Shankar followed him. In the light of the torch, they saw that the shrubs in the north-eastern side of their camp had been trampled down completely, as if a steamroller had passed by. Alvarez fired two shots in that direction.

There was no response.

While returning to the tent, both of them saw the footprints quite close to the campfire. Clear imprints of three toes.

The animal was not afraid of fire. Shankar wondered what would have happened if Alvarez had not woken up. The unknown terror would not have hesitated to enter their tent and it was no use imagining the consequences. Alvarez said, "You sleep, I will stand guard."

Shankar said, "No, you sleep, I'll stay awake."

Alvarez smiled weakly and said, "Are you crazy? You won't be able to do anything even if you are awake. Go to bed. Look, there is lightning in the distance, it will rain again. The night will be over soon, please sleep for some time. I think I'll have a cup of coffee."

With dawn came torrential rains, accompanied by the sound and fury of intense lightning. It continued throughout the day without any letup. Shankar felt as if it was Pralay, the final, deciding deluge that would drown the world. The God of Destruction had decided to obliterate the earth. The rain was so fierce that even Alvarez was downbeat, he did not talk of taking down the tent.

It stopped raining around five in the afternoon. Shankar felt it would have been better if the rain hadn't stopped, because, immediately, Alvarez instructed him to pack up and start. The easy going Bengali in Shankar felt there was no need to start at that odd hour, time was not all that valuable to them. But for Alvarez, there was no difference between day and night, rain and shine, new moon and full moon. That night, they climbed the mountain through the rain washed jungle by finding their way in the moonlight seeping through scattered clouds. After some time, Alvarez called from behind, "Shankar! Stop. Look ahead."

In the clear moonlight, Alvarez was looking through his field glasses at a mountain towards their left. Shankar took the field glasses from him and looked up. He could see the mountain pass. It wasn't far, it was within two miles to their left.

A beaming Alvarez said, "Have you seen the saddle? We won't stop now, we must reach there tonight. We'll camp on the saddle."

Shankar was at the end of his tether. He regretted his decision to join this relentless Portuguese on an expedition. But he knew that a basic rule in any expedition was that the leader could not be questioned, his orders had to be carried out without protest. There was no written code, but in all the major expeditions in history, this rule was followed. Shankar too would follow it.

When they reached the saddle at the crack of dawn, after a nonstop climb, Shankar did not have the energy to move one more step. The saddle was wider than three miles. At one place, there was a steep rise of two hundred feet and at another, within a mile, there was a descent of four to five hundred feet. The terrain was therefore not easy to negotiate. Part of the saddle was relatively plain, but such areas were covered by a jungle of bamboo grass, wild ginger plants and tall trees like erythronium and soapnut. There was a wide variety of orchids on the trees and baboons and monkeys everywhere.

After climbing down continuously for two more days, they crossed over to the valley on the other side of the main range of the Richtersveldts.

Shankar felt the jungle on this side was even more wild and

impenetrable. On the western coast of Africa, clouds which formed over the Atlantic Ocean are partly stopped by the Cameroon Mountains. The rest reach the southern face of the Richtersveldt Mountain. As a result, this region gets heavy rainfall and has a thick forest cover.

For fifteen days they searched for the river described by Alvarez in the dense jungles of that valley, but could not find it. They came across a number of rivulets, but every time Alvarez shook his head and said, "No, this is not the one."

Shankar said, "Shall we study the map carefully once again?"

By then, it had become quite clear that Alvarez's map was useless. He said, "I don't need a map. That river and valley are etched permanently in my memory, I will recognize the place the moment I see it. This is not it. This is not the valley we are looking for."

They had no choice. They had to keep searching.

A month passed. With March came the rainy season in West Africa. It was awful. Shankar had got a glimpse of the intensity of rain in these parts while crossing the Richtersveldt. A number of mighty streams cascaded down the mountain slope, they seemed determined to wash the valley away. There was no place to even pitch the tent. One night, a narrow stream in front of their tent turned into a strong rivulet and almost washed away their tent. Once again they survived because of Alvarez's alertness.

Time moved slowly.

One day, Shankar had an extraordinary experience that nearly killed him. Alvarez was cleaning his rifle in the tent. After that he was to cook. Shankar went into the jungle in search of game.

Alvarez had cautioned him to be extremely careful and not to leave the tent without a loaded rifle. Alvarez had also asked him to keep a compass tied to his wrist and leave signs on trees along the path so that he could find his way back to the tent. Otherwise, he would certainly be in trouble.

On that day, Shankar went deep inside the jungle in search of the springbok antelope. He had started in the morning. When he was tired, he sat down under a tree to take a breather. There were large trees everywhere and almost each one of them was completely covered with a creeper with small leaves. Nearby, by the side of a small waterhole, there were bushes with bright flowers.

After he sat there for some time, he felt a little uneasy. He could not understand what exactly caused his discomfort. But he did not feel like leaving the place. He was tired and the place was quite comfortable.

After a while, his body felt numb. He wondered if it was an attack of malaria. To overcome the feeling, he lit a cheroot. There was a pleasant, sweet smell in the air and Shankar liked it. After some time when he picked up the matchbox from the ground and put it into his pocket, he felt his arm did not belong to him, but to someone else, as it did not quite follow the commands of his brain.

Gradually, his entire body felt pleasantly numb. He wondered if there was any point in their expedition, the unending chase of a chimera. Wouldn't it be better to spend the rest of his life dreaming languidly under the pleasant shadows of this quiet forest? A part of his mind told him to get up immediately and return to their tent, otherwise he would be in serious trouble. But his numbness won the day. It was not exactly numbness, it was laced with the pleasures of a pleasant intoxication. The rest of the world became insignificant. The feeling spread over his entire body.

Shankar rested his head on a root and lay down comfortably. There were faint lines drawn by light and shade on the tall cottonwood trees, a wild owl was hooting for quite some time, the hoot became more and more indistinct ... He did not remember anything else.

By the time Alvarez discovered Shankar's unconscious body under the cottonwood tree after a long search, it was almost dark. Initially, Alvarez thought Shankar had been bitten by a snake, but he could not see any mark of snakebite on Shankar's body. Alvarez looked up and observed the surroundings. With his vast experience of tropical forests, he immediately realized what had happened. The creepers were poisonous. Some African tribesmen dip their arrowheads in the juice of this poison. The creeper has a pleasant smell, but if one breathes in too much of the poisoned air, one may get paralyzed, and may even die.

Brought back to their tent, Shankar was confined to bed for three days. His body was swollen. He had a splitting headache and his throat was dry all the time. Alvarez told him that if he had spent the whole night under the tree, it would have been difficult to save him.

Some more time passed. One day, Shankar noticed some yellow grains on the banks of a rivulet. Alvarez was a skilled prospector, he sieved the sand and extracted a few grains of gold. But he was not much enthused by the discovery. The quantity of gold was so meagre that it would not be worth the trouble. They would get about three ounces of gold from one tonne of the mineral.

Shankar said, "Still, instead of sitting idle, let's try to extract as much gold as possible. Even three ounces of gold is not something to be ignored!"

But what was a great discovery to Shankar was insignificant to the seasoned prospector in Alvarez. Besides, Shankar's concept of value was different from that of Alvarez. Ultimately, Shankar had to give up.

In the meantime, they wandered about in the forest for over a month. They camped at one place for a few days, then moved over to another. After searching the new area thoroughly, they shifted to yet another place. One day, they had just pitched their camp at a new site. Shankar returned to the tent in the afternoon after shooting a few birds. He found Alvarez smoking a cigar and looking worried.

Shankar said, "I think, when you yourself haven't been able to locate the river, we should go back."

Alvarez said, "The river can't fly away! It must be there, in some part of this forest."

"Then why can't we find it?"

"We are not searching properly."

"I don't understand, Alvarez! We have combed this forest over the last six months. If this is not searching properly, then what is?"

"But there is a problem, Shankar," Alvarez replied grimly. "I haven't told you something till now, thinking you might be scared. Come with me, I'll show you something."

Curious and anxious, Shankar followed Alvarez.

Alvarez went a little away from the tent. He stood under a large tree and said, "We have come here today, haven't we?"

Shankar was surprised to hear the question. He said, "Of course we have, why ask me?"

"Come closer and look at this trunk carefully."

Shankar saw someone had carved the letters D A with a knife on the soft bark of the tree. But the carving was not fresh, it was at least a month old!

Shankar had no idea how such an extraordinary thing could happen. He looked at Alvarez blankly. Alvarez said, "Don't you understand? About a month ago I myself marked the tree with my initials because I had a doubt. To you, all jungles look the same. Do you understand what this means? We are going around in a circle in the forest. When such a thing happens, it is very difficult to get out."

Shankar asked, "You mean to say we passed by this place a month ago?"

"Exactly. Such things happen in large forests and deserts. They are known as Death Circles. About a month ago, I suspected that we were trapped in one. I marked the tree to test if my hunch was correct. Today, I chanced upon this tree while I was out for a walk."

Shankar asked, "But what happened to our compass? How could we lose our way despite having the compass?"

Alvarez said, "I think our compass is not working. Possibly it was de-magnetized when we passed through the thunderstorm while crossing the Richtersveldt."

"So it is useless?"

"I think so."

Shankar realized that their situation was not exactly enviable. The maps were incorrect, their compass was out of order and on top of everything, they were trapped in a death circle. There was no one to help them, they had no food and it was risky to drink the water they found along the way. The only companion that never deserted them was the fear of an unfamiliar and terrible death. Jim Carter came in search of treasure and died in this cursed forest. No good could come out of this place.

But Alvarez was not a person to be cowed down. He trekked through the forest relentlessly, day after day. Shankar followed him, his bearings lost. Earlier he had tried to understand the geography of the place, but after he knew they were going round in a circle, he gave up.

After three days they reached a place where a smaller hill of the Richtersveldt range was at right angles to the main range. This hill was to the south of the main range. It was at least four thousand feet high. Towards further west, there was a still higher peak partly hidden by clouds. The valley between these two hills was about three miles wide and it was covered by dense jungles.

In the forest, there were three to four distinct layers in the vegetation. In the top layer, there were parasites and moss. The middle layer consisted of large trees. The lowest layer had small plants, shrubs and bushes. Sunlight did not enter that jungle.

Alvarez decided to camp in the valley, but did not enter the dense jungle. In the evening, they discussed their situation while drinking coffee. They had run out of food, they had had no sugar for quite some time. They had coffee for a few more days. A little wheat flour was still left, and that was about all. They still had the flour because they rarely used it. They depended almost entirely on the meat of wild animals, but as they were not carrying an ammunition factory with them, they could not expect to go on hunting forever.

While they talked, Shankar looked at the distant mountain

peak that was playing hide and seek with the clouds. Suddenly, when the clouds cleared for a short while, they could see the peak clearly. It looked rather strange. It was as if the tip of a kulfi had been partly bitten off.

Alvarez said, "From here, Bulawayo or Salisbury is within four to five hundred miles towards the south-east. In between, there is a desert that is about two hundred miles wide. Towards west, the coast is only three hundred miles away, but the forests in the Portuguese West Africa are impregnable, let's not count on that option. Now, the only way out is that either you or I go to Salisbury or Bulawayo and return with bullets and food. We also need compasses."

For Shankar, it was a stroke of luck that he heard this from Alvarez. Fate does strange things to human beings. We often fail to understand their significance. It was sheer good fortune that Shankar heard the names of the towns Bulawayo and Salisbury and their direction and approximate distance from this place. Later, he thanked Alvarez countless times for mentioning these facts.

Their discussion did not proceed further. Both of them were tired and went to bed early.

n the middle of the night Shankar was awakened by a strange noise. The jungles seemed to be gripped by a huge turbulence. Alvarez too was sitting up on his bed. They listened carefully and what they heard was truly mysterious. They had no clue to what was happening.

Shankar switched on his torch and was about to leave the tent, but Alvarez stopped him. He said, "Don't rush out of the tent at night in these unknown jungles. I have cautioned you several times. Besides, where's your rifle?"

It was absolutely dark outside. What they saw in the torchlight was beyond comprehension.

Wild animals were running desperately, trampling on bushes and small plants. They came out of the mountain forest on the west and ran towards the hill on the east. There were hyenas, baboons and wild buffaloes. Two leopards passed close by them. More were coming … there were hordes of them … Male and female Colobuses came in large groups carrying their babies. It seemed the animals sensed an impending disaster and were fleeing for their lives. Simultaneously, Shankar and Alvarez heard a rumbling at a distance. It was subdued, dull, like the rumbling of thunder. Or perhaps, at a place far away, a thousand drums were being played simultaneously.

They wondered what it was all about. They looked at each other, astounded. Alvarez said, "Let's make the fire bigger, otherwise these animals will trample down our tent."

The number of animals increased with time. Above them, the birds too were flying away, leaving their nests. A large herd of springbok antelope came within ten yards of them. But Shankar and Alvarez were too confused – so much so that they forgot to shoot. They had never seen anything like this.

Shankar was about to ask Alvarez something, when catastrophe struck. At least, that's how it seemed to Shankar. The ground beneath them shook violently and they were thrown off their feet.

While getting up, Alvarez said, "Earthquake!"

The next moment, they were dumbfounded to see that the impenetrable darkness of the night had vanished and the forest was lit up as if by a million electric lights. Within seconds, there was a deafening noise that was louder than a thousand thunderclaps. As if the earth was torn apart and the sky had exploded. It seemed as if a thousand thunderbolts had clapped together somewhere near them.

Something strange was happening at the odd looking peak of the mountain. An immense fire leapt out of it. In that dazzling, eerie light, the entire mountain forest looked red. Clouds of fire gushed out of the peak and rose over two thousand feet in the sky. At the same time, the sickening smell of sulphur filled the air.

Alvarez looked at the peak and said in awe, "A volcano! Santa Ana Grazia de Cordova."

The scene that unfolded before them was terrible, but, at the same time, fascinatingly beautiful. They could not take their eyes off it for quite some time. Shankar felt someone had lit innumerable fireworks on the truncated peak of the mountain. At times, the glowing red clouds came down, and all of a sudden, whipped up again by thousands of feet. The sight was accompanied by the sound of thousands of bombs exploding simultaneously.

The ground was shaking so violently that it was impossible to stand up straight. After falling down several times, Shankar entered the tent with faltering steps. A small, trembling animal was lying curled up on his bed. It looked like a puppy. Confused by the torchlight, it looked at Shankar with its glowing eyes. Alvarez entering the tent said, "A leopard cub. Let it be, it's looking for shelter."

Neither of them had seen a volcanic eruption before, so they had no idea about what was to follow. Before Alvarez could finish, they heard a noise of a heavy object falling somewhere near their tent. They came out and saw a large piece of burning red hot rock had fallen in a bush close at hand. The bush caught fire immediately. Alvarez said in an excited voice, "Hurry up, Shankar, we have to run. Take down the tent, immediately!"

By the time they could fold the tent, four or five more balls

of fire fell around them. The sulphur in the air made it difficult for them to breathe.

Run … Run … Run … For two hours they ran, partly carrying, partly dragging their things. They reached the bottom of the hill towards the east, but there was no respite from the pungent smell. After half an hour, the shower of burning rocks started there too. They were forced to climb up the mountain slope, overcoming thick shrubs. By dawn, they reached a height of about two thousand feet. Panting heavily, they sat down under a tall tree.

After the sun rose, the glow of the volcanic outburst faded, but the sound increased and so did the intensity of the shower of rocks. It was not rocks alone, a fine dust of ash was raining from the sky. In no time a thin layer of ash collected on the leaves all around. The eruption continued through the day.

It was night once again. The massive trees in the valley below them were completely burnt and destroyed. At night, the frightful but gorgeous spectacle came to life again. The sky and the forest were lit up by the fire cauldron within the volcano. As far as they could see, the mountain forests all around were red. The shower of rocks stopped. But the red clouds glowed the same way.

Around midnight, they woke up from their sleep on hearing a huge explosion. They watched the mountain peak in awe. The top of the fiery volcano had blown off. The valley between the two hills was completely destroyed by ash, molten lava and the shower of burning rocks. Alvarez was injured by a flying rock. Their tent caught fire. Behind them, a high branch of a tree broke and fell down as it was hit by a piece of huge rock.

Shankar thought that, but for them, no one would have known that such a gigantic natural disaster had taken place in this desolate forest. The civilized world did not even know of the existence of this volcano. Perhaps no one would believe them when they narrated this experience.

In the morning, they could clearly see the notches on the top edge of the volcano. The serrated edge looked like the top of a blown out candle. Someone had had another bite of the kulfi!

Alvarez verified his map and said, "This map does not show a volcano here. Perhaps this volcano erupted after a long time. But the name of the mountain given in the map is significant."

Shankar asked, "What is it?"

Alvarez said, "Oldonio Lengai. In the old Zulu language, it means The Seat of the Fire God. From the name, it seems, earlier people of this area knew of the existence of the volcano. Perhaps it was dormant for a hundred years or more."

Shankar, a son of India, unconsciously touched his forehead with joined hands. O God of Fire, I bow to you. You have allowed me to watch your dance of annihilation. I thank you for bestowing upon me this honour. A hundred diamond mines pale into insignificance compared to this spectacle. It is the ultimate reward for all the hardship that I have gone through. I do not crave for anything more.

lvarez did not consider it safe to stay so close to the volcano. They avoided the smoking Oldonio Lengai and went further west. The dense jungle in that area was not even singed by the fire. On the contrary, after the rains, it was lush green with fresh plants and bushes. There were many springs and rivulets, but the river they were looking for continued to elude them.

This time they came to a place where there were many granite and limestone hills. Most of these hills had caves of various sizes. The place looked different from the landscape commonly seen in the Richtersveldts. The forest was not too thick here, although many tall trees were scattered around the hills.

They made camp on a high granite hillock. Shankar kept feeling there was something wrong with the place. He had a vague sense of discomfort and a premonition of danger, but he neither understood what was wrong, nor could he explain his feelings to Alvarez.

After a few days, Alvarez said, "All our efforts are in vain, we are still in the death circle. Today I saw the tree with my initials again. But you know that we have been keeping to the west for the last fifteen days. How did we reach the same tree?"

Shankar did not understand Alvarez's logic. If they were moving in a circle, how did they reach this valley of low hills and caves? As far as he could remember, they hadn't come here earlier. Alvarez explained to him that the tree with his initials was only two miles away in the west. Earlier, when they found the tree, they did not move towards east, so they never came to this place, although they came quite close by.

Shankar said, "What is to be done now?"

"Tonight, I will climb up to the top of a tall tree. I'll be able to make out the directions by observing the stars. You stay in the tent."

That night, Shankar was alone in the tent, reading Bankimchandra's *Raajsingha*. This was the only book he had brought from home. Although he had read the novel many times, he read it again whenever he got time.

Bharotborsho was far away, and so were Chittor, Mewar and the wars between the Mughals and the Rajputs! In this dense, unknown, African forest, they seemed to be imaginary lands out of a fiction.

He heard footsteps outside the tent. At first Shankar thought Alvarez was returning to the tent. But he realized immediately they couldn't be the footsteps of a human being. Such a sound maybe produced if a lame man walked with a heavy weight tied to his feet. Shankar had Alvarez's Winchester repeater with him. He crouched at the entrance of the tent with the rifle. The footsteps stopped for sometime. Then the sound moved from the right of the tent to the left. Shankar could hear a large animal breathing. It was exactly like what they had heard while crossing the mountain. Shankar lost his nerve and pressed the trigger – not once, but twice.

Immediately, Alvarez responded from the top of a tree, firing his pistol twice. Alvarez thought Shankar was in danger, otherwise he would not have shot twice. Shankar also realized Alvarez might return to the tent immediately.

In the meantime, the animal fled after hearing so many gunshots. Shankar could no longer hear its footsteps. He came out as he wanted to send a signal to Alvarez with the torchlight, telling him that he was all right. But before he could do anything, he heard two more pistol shots and a muffled cry.

Shankar ran towards the sound. A short distance away, he found Alvarez lying under a tree. Shining the torchlight on him, Shankar trembled in fear and shock. Alvarez was covered in blood, his head was at an unusual angle to his torso. His jacket had been torn to shreds.

Shankar sat down and held Alvarez's head in his arms. He called, "Alvarez! Alvarez!"

There was no response. Alvarez's lips quivered, he wanted to say something, but could not. His eyes were fixed at Shankar, but they looked blank. Even if he could see, he was unconcerned about what he saw.

Shankar carried Alvarez to the tent and gave him water to drink. While taking off his coat, Shankar noticed that a large chunk of flesh had been ripped off from his shoulder. He had lacerations on his back too. It seemed an unusually strong animal had torn his back to shreds with its nails or teeth.

Shankar had also noticed the footprints of the animal on the soft ground.

They had only three toes.

Alvarez's condition did not improve during the night. He neither spoke on his own, nor responded to Shankar's questions. By early morning, he regained consciousness for a short while. He had a dazed, vacant look and did not seem to recognize Shankar. Then he closed his eyes again. In the afternoon, he was delirious, he talked possibly in his mother tongue, and Shankar could not understand a word of what he said. A little before evening, he suddenly looked at Shankar and from his look, Shankar knew Alvarez had recognized him. Then Alvarez spoke in English. "Shankar, why are you waiting? Take the tent down, we have to start." He lifted his right hand in an attempt to show him something. He said, "An enormous treasure is lying in that cave. I can see it clearly! Can't you? Let's start. Don't wait any more. Take the tent down."

Those were the last words of Alvarez.

For a long time, Shankar could not move a muscle. Evening came. Slowly, the entire forest was drowned in darkness.

He came out of his trance, got up hurriedly and lit a fire. Then he loaded both the rifles, took aim towards the entrance of the tent and sat beside Alvarez's body.

Later in the night, another torrential rain started. Water seeped through the tent and drenched everything. But Shankar was in such a state that he hardly noticed anything. In the last few months, he had developed a deep admiration and affection for Alvarez. Shankar was greatly impressed by his fearlessness, his determination, his tremendous patience, his courage... Alvarez was like a father figure to him.

But more than anything else, Shankar found it inconsolable that Alvarez was killed by the same mysterious creature that had killed Jim Carter.

As the night wore on, an overwhelming fear gripped Shankar. He was being stalked by a dangerous, unknown harbinger of death, an animal shrouded in mystery. No one knew when and how it would attack. There was no way Shankar could relax, he stayed awake through the night.

He would not forget the terror of that dreadful night till his last breath. Raindrops on leaves and a nonstop storm drowned out all other sounds. He heard deafening noises of massive trees being uprooted in the storm. Alone in the forest, he watched the black trunks of the trees that looked like ghosts. Fireflies glowed, despite the rain.

He was keeping vigil over his friend's body. He was in a hopeless situation, but could not afford to panic. He had to be calm and in control of his mind. Otherwise, fear itself would kill him. In his desperate attempt to drive away fear, he concentrated hard on the rifles. One was a Winchester, and the other a Mannlicher, both were loaded. Shankar told himself that there was no animal made of flesh and blood that could enter his tent unharmed.

Fear and danger make one courageous. Fear is the key to fearlessness. Shankar sat alertly throughout the night. The next morning he buried the body of Alvarez under a tall tree. He made a cross by tying two branches with strong creepers, and placed it on Alvarez's grave.

Among Alverez's papers, there was a faded diploma from the Oporto Mining School in his name. Alvarez had graduated from the school with honours. From the way he talked, Shankar had often suspected that he was not another uneducated vagabond in search of a fortune.

Far away from human habitation, in the middle of that desolate, dense forest, the tired Alvarez's search for treasure had ended. It is not the lure of treasure that motivates men like him. For them, supreme happiness means seeing the world and facing dangers. Even Kuber's treasures would not keep them in one place for long.

It was a befitting mausoleum for the fearless explorer. Trees of an ancient forest would provide shade over his grave. Lions, gorillas, hyenas would stand guard at night. Above all, the majestic Richtersveldt Mountain, with its peaks venturing into the kingdom of clouds, would watch over Alvarez till eternity.

TEN

Another day passed. The utter hopelessness of the situation made Shankar desperate. He knew that if he panicked, there was little chance of leaving the forest alive. For two days, he stayed in the tent and pondered over his options, concentrating deeply. He made his plans. All of a sudden, he remembered what Alvarez had casually mentioned in a different context – Salisbury! Five hundred miles from there! Towards the south-east.

Salisbury, the capital of South Rhodesia. Somehow he had to reach Salisbury. An astrologer had told him he would live long. Shankar refused to accept defeat, he would not die in this godforsaken place.

Shankar studied the maps carefully. A map drawn by the forest survey team of the Portuguese government, a map of coastal Africa prepared by the marine surveyors and another drawn by the explorer Sir Phillipo De Phillip. Besides, there was a worn out, faded sepia sketch prepared by Alvarez and signed by Jim Carter. When Alvarez was alive, Shankar did not care to study these maps. Now his life depended on interpreting them correctly. He had to find the shortest route to Salisbury. He had to estimate the latitude and longitude of his location and escape from the maze of the Richtersveldt Mountain. Everything depended on these maps.

After studying the maps for quite some time, he realized none of them gave any details of these mountain forests, except the sketch drawn by Alvarez and Carter. But even that was incomplete. Besides, Alvarez and Carter had probably thought that if their map found its way to someone else's hands, their treasure would be stolen. They had used many cryptic signs while drawing the map. In short, Shankar could not clearly read that map either.

Four days after Alvarez's death, Shankar started walking roughly towards the east. Before leaving that place, he made a wreath of wild flowers and put it on Alvarez's grave.

There is something called Bushcraft which one has to learn in order to survive in large, dense forests. Shankar had learnt a bit of these tricks under the tutelage of Alvarez, but he was not sure if he could cross the forest alone. He had to depend entirely on his destiny. If his luck favoured him, he would cross safely. If it did not, then death. He prayed and hoped god would show him the way.

He crossed a few high and low hills. The forest was dense in places and relatively light elsewhere. But all around, there were tall, massive trees. Shankar knew that if he reached fields with tall elephant grass, he would have come out of the forest, because elephant or tussock grass does not grow in dense forests. But he saw no sign of these – there were only tall trees with undergrowth.

The first day ended in a denser jungle. Shankar had left behind most of his things. He carried only Alvarez's Mannlicher rifle, a substantial quantity of bullets, the canteen, the torch, the maps, the compass, his watch, a blanket and some medicines. He also took a hammock with him. Although their tent was very light, Shankar had felt it would be impossible to carry it, and had left it behind.

He hung the hammock at a fairly high level between two trees. He also lit a fire to ward off animals. He lay down in the hammock and remained awake with the rifle by his side. He could not sleep for two reasons. Firstly, a swarm of mosquitoes made his life miserable and secondly, a leopard started moving about shortly after sunset. In the darkness, its eyes glowed like two pellets of fire. It went away when Shankar flashed the torch, but came closer after some time. Shankar was afraid that the leopard, a cunning animal, would jump upon the hammock if he fell asleep.

Besides, there was a wide variety of noises made by animals. Shankar could not sleep a wink. Once, he had dozed off, but suddenly he heard some small children laughing nearby. He got up with a start wondering how there could be children in that forest. The next moment he recalled Alvarez telling him once that the screech of a kind of baboon sounded exactly like children's laughter.

In the morning, he got down from the tree and started walking. Aeroplane pilots use a term – Flying blind. Shankar

trekked through the forest in the same fashion, depending on, more than anything else, his fate. He was not too sure in which direction he was going and, as a result, lost his bearings within two days. He realized how difficult it was to stick to a particular direction while walking through a large and dense jungle. There are countless trees, one sees only tree trunks all around. Above one's head is an endless canopy of branches, leaves and creepers. One does not see the stars, the moon or the sun. The sunlight is diffused, it is twilight throughout the day. For mile after mile after mile, the jungle looks the same. The compass too, was useless. There was no way he could follow any definite direction.

On the fifth day, he stopped at the bottom of a hill for rest. There was an enormous cavern nearby. A narrow stream flowed out from the entrance of the cavern and meandered into the jungle.

Shankar had not seen such a huge cave earlier. As curiosity got the better of him, he left his backpack behind and entered the cavern. There was some light at the entrance – but inside, it was absolutely dark. He moved cautiously in the light from his torch and after a while, reached a place where the cave bifurcated into two.

Shankar looked up in the torchlight

and found the roof of the cave was quite high there. Nature's own chandeliers hung from the ceiling in the shape of white stalactite formations of calcium carbonate.

Water trickled down the walls of the cave in many places. Shankar entered the cave on his right. The entrance to this was narrow, but gradually, it became wider. Beneath his feet the ground was soft wet earth, not rock. In the torchlight, he saw that the cave was triangular in shape. At another corner of the triangle was one more opening. On entering through that opening, Shankar reached a narrow passage that had high walls of rocks on both sides. This cave was narrow and serpentine. As he meandered along it, Shankar went further and further into the cave.

After about two hours, Shankar felt it was time to go back. But on his way back, he could not find the triangular cave. He did not understand how he could miss it. He was sure that the narrow, tunnel-like cave emerged from the triangular cave. Logically, when he walked back to the beginning of the narrow cave, he should have reached the triangular cave. But he did not.

After searching for some time, Shankar felt nervous. Had he lost his way? It would be the end if he had.

He sat down and tried to regain his poise. He told himself that he just couldn't afford to panic, he had to keep a cool head. He recalled that Alvarez had taught him to leave marks along the path when he went to an unknown place, so that he could trace his way back. He had forgotten this basic lesson. What could he do now?

Shankar was in a dilemma whether to light his torch or not. If the cells ran out, he would be doomed. But, it was pitch-dark within the cave and he could not move even one step forward in that darkness. There was no question of finding his way.

The day got over. The watch showed seven pm. The torchlight was turning red. It was musty and hot inside the cave, and Shankar had no drinking water with him. The water seeping down the stone wall was bitter and caustic. Even that bitter water flowed only in trickles, Shankar had to lick it off the surface of the wall.

It would have become dark outside, the watch showed seven thirty. Eight, nine, ten. Shankar was still searching. The flashlight had been on almost continuously since three in the afternoon. By now the cells were weak and the light, dim. Shankar became frantic. He knew he could nurse hopes as long as the torch managed to throw some light, but without light, there was only one prospect – he would rot in that hell. Even Alvarez could not have found his way in that impenetrable darkness.

Shankar switched off the torch and sat down on a boulder… Yes, perhaps he could come out of this death trap if he had spare batteries, but there was little he could do without light. Once he thought he would wait for the morning and then start again. The next moment he remembered day or night did not make the slightest difference inside the cave.

He started walking in the darkness itself, feeling the wall with his hands. He cursed himself for not carrying new cells while entering the cavern. At the very least, he should have carried a matchbox!

According to the watch, it was morning. But there was no hint of light in that eternal darkness. Perhaps he was destined to die a wretched death in that dark cave, perhaps he would not see daylight again. Africa had not been satiated with the sacrifice of the life of Alvarez, it wanted Shankar's too.

Three days and three nights passed. Shankar had chewed on the insoles of his boots. There was not even a cockroach or rat or scorpion to offer him an apology of a meal. Shankar felt he was slowly becoming insane, he had no control over what he did, and his mind no longer registered what happened around him. He was clear about only one thing, he had to get out of the cave, he had to see the light of the day. So he went on groping in darkness with his feeble body, perhaps he would go on doing so till his death.

At some point, he fell into an exhausted slumber. He had no idea how long he slept. That unrelenting darkness effaced concepts like day, night, hours, minutes and seconds. Perhaps his eyesight was weakening. He was not too sure.

After sleeping for sometime, he felt slightly better. He got up and started walking again. He was a disciple of Diego Alvarez, he would not die a passive death … He would go on fighting till his last breath.

It baffled Shankar that under his feet, he no longer felt the stream he had found at the entrance of the cavern … At some point of time, while going around in the maze of the cave, he had deviated from the stream. There might be an escape route if he found it again, because it flowed out of the cave. But during the last three days, he had not found any water underfoot, let alone the stream. The thirst was killing, Shankar had been licking the caustic water from the walls of the cave. His tongue had swollen from the effort and it had done nothing to quench his thirst. If anything, it had increased it.

Shankar started searching for moss on the walls, so that he

could eat some and save his life. But even that was not available. The rocks were barren, with the exception of occasional thin layers of calcium carbonate. There were no plants like moss, or fungal growths like mushrooms. With absolutely no sunlight, no form of life could germinate in that cave.

Another day passed and night came. Despite all his efforts, Shankar was not any better off. He had become totally dispirited by then. How long could he go on and what was the purpose of it all? It made no difference, there was no way out. Where was he going in that terrible darkness and in that deafening silence? It seemed as if the earth was dead, as if the last dance of destruction had put out the sun. In that timeless, lifeless, soundless, desolate universe, Shankar was the only living creature.

If he could not find a way out quickly he was bound to go mad.

ELEVEN

Shankar dozed off for a while, or perhaps he lost consciousness. When he got up, his watch showed twelve. Probably midnight. He pulled himself up and started walking again. After a while he found his path was blocked by a stone wall. He switched on the torch for a moment and saw in its red light a barrier that stood at right angles to the wall along which he had been walking.

Suddenly, he heard the faint noise of flowing water. He pricked up his ears and listened with rapt attention.

Yes. It was actually the sound of a small spring flowing over pebbles and rocks. After listening carefully, he felt the sound came from the other side of the stone wall. He put his ear on the wall and decided it was indeed so. He switched on the dim flashlight for a moment once again and looked for an opening to go over to the other side of the wall. He saw a low and narrow crevice. After crawling through the opening for quite a distance, his hands touched water. He carefully stretched upward to find that he could even stand there. He stood up. After moving a few steps he found himself standing in ankle-deep ice-cold water ...

In that total darkness, he bent down and drank to his heart's content. Then, in the faint light of the torch, he checked the direction of the current. Generally these streams flow out of caves, and not the other way round. He moved with the flow of the water for quite some time. The stream meandered along. After some distance, Shankar felt it had branched into three or four sub-streams that flowed in different directions.

Shankar was in a fix. With a quick flash of the torchlight he saw the streamlets flowing in different directions. He recalled Alvarez's teaching; if he did not leave signs from here onwards, he might get into trouble again. He bent down in search of something that could be used as markers and found many pebbles on both sides of the shallow stream. The ice-cold water flowed over these pebbles.

Shankar filled his pockets with the pebbles and decided to explore each streamlet till the end. He moved forward leaving pairs of pebbles by the side of the water. After some distance, the stream once again split into a number of smaller ones. At every point of bifurcation he made a sign of "S" with the pebbles.

Some of the streams seemed to flow back to the point from where Shankar had started. In spite of leaving signs, Shankar found the whole thing most confusing. Once he stepped upon something very cold. With a flash of his torch, he saw a huge python that lay curled up beside the water. The python came out of its slumber and looked at him with its beady eyes. Fortunately for Shankar, the torchlight confused it, otherwise, he might have lost his life. Shankar knew that pythons were exceedingly dangerous. He had heard instances of men fighting lions or tigers with bare hands, but even the strongest of them could not escape from the grip of a python. If the snake had caught him, it would have been the end.

Presently, a new terror gripped Shankar. It was quite possible that another python was lying in wait for him! He examined a couple of streamlets with the help of his marks, but he came back to the main point of distribution of the streamlets, which he had marked with a cross. He once again followed a course that seemed to be the main distributary. After walking for some time, he realized even that stream split into many smaller streamlets. In some places, the ceiling of the cave was so low that he had to bend down and walk like a hunchback.

Suddenly, Shankar saw, perhaps with the last glimmer of his fading flashlight, that he was in a triangular cave. The same triangular cave, in the search for which he had nearly died a terrible death. At last he was back to the triangular cave ... Soon, he saw stars framed in the dark entrance to the cavern. Now he was safe. The end of another ordeal!

When Shankar came out of the cavern, it was three in the morning. The jungle was not too thick there, the sky above shone with millions of gleaming stars. After coming out of the hell the cave turned out to be, the clear starry sky seemed as bright as an illuminated street of a metropolis. Shankar bowed down and thanked god for this unexpected reprieve.

Dawn arrived and sunlight caressed the trees. Shankar did not want to continue in that ungodly place even for another second. He had one pebble left in his pocket. Instead of throwing it away, he kept it as a memento of his dreadful experience in the cave.

The next day, he came across elephant grass, and before evening, he crossed the threshold of the forest and reached an open space. That night, Shankar studied the maps for a long time. The flat open land in front of him stretched three hundred miles, till the banks of the Zambezi river. A part of these three hundred miles, almost a hundred and seventy five, fell in the northern fringes of the Kalahari desert, a terrible, desolate place without water or tracks. Alvarez had noted from a military map that if, instead of following a particular route along the north-eastern boundary, one tried to cross the desert across the middle, one stood no chance of survival. The desert was marked on the map as the Land of Thirst! Once he reached Rhodesia it would be relatively easier, as there would be human habitation there.

Shankar's courage came to the fore once again. Although he knew how daunting his task was, he refused to be cowed down. Alvarez had offered to cross this desert alone and bring back bullets and food from Salisbury. Shankar refused to accept that he could not do what a sixty two year old man could.

But courage and fearlessness are often poor substitutes for knowledge and experience. Shankar could not interpret maps and identify directions of places. The military map marked two oases with their latitudes and longitudes. Alvarez used to work out the latitude and longitude of a place by solving a complex problem involving the Magnetic North and True North. Shankar had seen him doing so, but had not learnt the tricks from him.

Therefore, he was necessarily at the mercy of fate. He recognized this simple fact and, leaving his future to chance, prepared to cross the frightening desert. Therefore, the obvious thing happened. Within two days he lost his bearings completely. He passed by a point which was only three miles to the north of an oasis. An experienced traveller could have found it blindfolded by reading the maps. But Shankar could not. Although at that time he had nearly run out of water. His life would be in peril if he could not find water immediately.

To begin with, there was only wide open land with cacti and euphorbias and occasional hillocks of granite. Gradually, the trek became exceedingly difficult. Shankar had no food or water, no trail to follow, and he could nurse no hope of meeting another human being. He walked towards the horizon for days together, a hopeless journey towards nowhere. Above him, the sun glowed like a ball of fire, beneath his feet, the sand was like burning charcoal. The sun rose and set, the stars appeared and merged into the morning sky, the moon rose and set. The desert lizards made a monotonous noise, and so did the crickets at night.

There are no milestones in deserts. Shankar had no idea about the distance he had covered. His food consisted of a bird or two, at times the desert buzzard, the meat of which was tasteless and tough. Even a scorpion caught while crossing a hill was considered a delicacy and a matter of good luck, although the scorpion was poisonous enough to kill a man.

After two days of suffering without water, Shankar found

water in a crevice in a hill. But the water was red and insects were floating in it. The swollen carcass of an animal lay by the edge of the water. Shankar drank as much of that water as he could. That dirty water saved his life.

One miserable day followed another. Shankar lost count of days and weeks. He was exhausted and worn out. He did not know where exactly he was heading. All that he knew was he had to keep moving forward. Ahead of him lay Bharotborsho and his Bangladesh.

Then he reached the edge of the real Kalahari Desert. Shankar watched it from a distance and shivered in silent terror. He wondered how anyone could cross that simmering wilderness on foot. Only sand dunes stood out in that tawny, featureless ocean of sand. The afternoon sun seemed to burn the barren earth. Even on the boundary of that desert, the thermometer showed a temperature of a hundred and twenty seven degrees Fahrenheit in the shade.

The maps clearly stated it was impossible to cross the desert except by a route along its north-eastern boundary, as there was absolutely no water elsewhere. That did not mean plenty of water was available along the north-eastern route either, but after gaps of thirty, seventy and ninety miles there were three springs where water seeped out through clefts in the ground. These springs were hidden in folds of hills. It was not easy to find them. To make it easier to find the springs, the army map gave their latitudes and longitudes.

Shankar knew he would not be able to work out the latitude and longitude of a place. He had star-charts and the sextant, but he did not know how to use them. But he was desperate.

Shankar is referring to the pre-Partition Bengal which was then referred to as **Bangladesh**.

He did his best to keep to the north-eastern edge of the desert.

On the third day, Shankar discovered a spring by sheer chance. The water was muddy and almost boiling, but to Shankar it tasted sweet and wonderful. From there on, the desert turned still more dangerous. There was no sign of plants or any other living organism. Earlier, in the night, his torchlight used to attract a few insects, but over time, even insects were not to be seen.

The days were terribly hot and the nights bitterly cold. In the early morning, the cold was freezing, but Shankar could not light a fire as there was no firewood. Within a few days, he ran out of water again. In that vast ocean of sand, finding a three feet wide spring was even more difficult than finding a particular grain of sand.

That evening, Shankar was frantic with thirst. By then he had realized that attempting to cross that Kalahari Desert all alone was akin to committing suicide slowly and painfully. But he was caught in a situation from where he could not even go back.

Climbing a high dune, he could see only tawny sand dunes rising gently towards the east. Although the sun had set, the sky still had an orange tinge. There was a small hillock a little away from where he stood, and from that distance, Shankar thought he saw a cave in the hillock. Such small hillocks of granite were common in the area. They are called Kopje in Rhodesia and Transvaal, which literally means small hills. Shankar took shelter in the cave for the night to keep the cold at bay.

What followed was strange.

TWELVE

Shankar still had two dozen new batteries. He entered the cave and lit his torch. He found it small, almost like a room. The floor was littered with small stones. Shankar was startled by what he saw in one corner of the cave. It was a small wooden barrel. It was perplexing. How could there be a barrel in such a place?

He took a few steps towards the barrel and got a shock.

Beside the wall of the cave lay a human skeleton with its skull turned towards the wall. Pieces of black rug were lying around it, possibly the remnants of a woollen jacket. Both the boots were still on its feet. And a rusted gun lay beside it.

Next to the barrel was a corked bottle, with a piece of paper inside. Shankar took out the paper and found something written in English.

Shankar was about to shake the barrel to check if it contained anything, when he heard a hiss from under it. His blood froze. The next moment, a snake flashed its hood about four feet above ground. Perhaps it waited for a fraction of a second before striking, and the delay saved Shankar's life. His rifle boomed quick as lightning. The head of the huge sand viper was mangled by the bullet, blood and flesh splashed on the barrel and the wall. Alvarez had taught him to always keep a weapon ready. That lesson had saved Shankar's life many a time.

It was a miraculous escape in more senses than one. On examining the barrel, Shankar found it still contained a little water. The black water looked more like ink, but it was water all the same. Shankar lifted the small barrel and drained the entire dirty, stinking water into his mouth. He examined the dead viper in torchlight. It was exactly seven and a half feet long and quite heavy. This snake, a dangerously poisonous one, usually lies buried in the desert sand, with its head jutting out.

Then Shankar unfolded the piece of paper and read it. In the bottle he also found the small pencil with which the message had been written. The message read,

I am close to my death. Tonight will be the last night of my life. If after my death anyone happens to take shelter in this cave while crossing this desert, this paper would possibly fall in his hands.

My donkey died in the desert two days ago. There was still a barrel of water on its back. I have carried the barrel into this cave, although I am sick. I have a high temperature and can hardly lift my head. Even otherwise, I was exceedingly weak after starving for days.

I am twenty six years old. I am Attilio Gatti, of the Gatti family of Florence. The famous sailor Rigolino Cavalcanti Gatti, who fought the Turks in the Battle of Lepanto, was my ancestor.

I studied in the universities of Rome and Pisa. But we were a family of sailors. In the end my love for the seas made a vagabond of me.

I was on my way to the Dutch Indies when our ship sank off the coast of West Africa. Seven of us somehow swam ashore. The forests are extremely dense on the western coast of Africa. We took shelter in a hamlet of the Shefu tribe in the jungles where we stayed for two months. In that village, we happened to hear the story of an enormous diamond reserve. They told us the reserve was in an exceedingly dense mountain forest to the east of the village.

We decided to go after the diamond deposit, however difficult the task might be. The men elected me as their leader. We trekked through dense jungles in search of that unknown destination. No one from the village agreed to accompany us. They said they had never been to the place and did not know where exactly it was situated. They also believed the forest was protected by a demigod and that no one could bring back diamonds from there.

But we were not to be easily discouraged. On the way, we faced terrible hardship. The journey took its toll, two members of our team died on the way. The other four did not want to proceed further. But I, their leader, belong to the Gatti family and have not learnt to turn my back. I know I have to move ahead as long as I am alive. I refused to return.

I cannot write any further, I know that the formless messenger of death will come for me tonight. Serino Lagrano is a very beautiful lake. Our family's mansion, Castillo Rigolini is on the bank of the lake. Even from this distance, I can smell the sweet oranges in the orchards by the banks of Serino Lagrano. I can hear the pleasant chime of the silver bell of the small church at the bottom of the hill.

What rubbish am I writing, I must be delirious. Let me jot down the essential points before it is too late. After all, how much longer am I going to write?

We did reach that mountain and the unusually dense forest. The source of the river on whose shores diamonds are found is in a huge and dangerous cave. I entered the cave alone and found innumerable diamonds on the riverbed within that cave. Each one of them was a transparent tetrahedron crystal with a tinge of yellow. Such beautiful diamonds cannot be found in the gem markets of London and Amsterdam.

In that cave, in the dim light of a smoking torch I saw from a distance the demigod that protected that mountain forest. It was truly frightening. It did not come close to me possibly because I was carrying a burning torch. I think the myth that a phantom is the protector of the diamond reserve has spread because it lives in that cave.

But the discovery of diamonds turned out to be a curse! And it was a mistake to tell my companions about the diamonds. When I entered the cave for the second time along with them, I could not find the diamonds! The darkness in that cave was impenetrable, our torches were not bright enough to dispel that dark. Secondly, the river had many distributaries, I could not identify the stream that flowed over diamonds.

My companions were deck hands. They were brutes. They thought I wanted to cheat them and make off with the diamonds alone. I did not know what conspiracy they hatched … the next evening the four of them together attacked me with knives. But they underestimated Attilio Gatti. I have the blood of Rigolini Cavalcanti Gatti, who killed many such barbarians in the Battle of Lepanto. When I was a cadet in the Military Academy of Santa Catalina, I wounded the best fencer, Antonio Dreifus, in a knife duel. My knife put two of them out of the way, and the other two were badly injured. I too was wounded in the skirmish. The two injured scoundrels died that very night. I felt I should not go into that cave again as I couldn't have found the diamond reserve in the maze of that cave. Besides, I was badly injured, I had to reach the civilized world. I started towards the east with the Dutch colony as my destination. But I can't go any further. They had stabbed me in the abdomen and the wound has got infected. I have fever too. I wonder why human beings are so greedy. They were my companions, the thought of cheating them had not once crossed my mind.

I am the owner of the greatest diamond reserve in the world, because I have risked my life to discover the place. I am sure that the gentleman who reads this message will be a civilized man and a Christian. I entreat him to give me a proper Christian burial. In exchange of that act of kindness, I bequeath the diamond reserve to him. Even Queen Sheba's treasures would pale into insignificance compared to that deposit.

I am going to die … but that's okay. There is nothing I can do about it. But what a terrible desert, one doesn't even hear crickets

chirping. I never thought there were such desolate places in this world. Tonight, Serino Lagrano and the poplars around it are coming back to my mind time and again. Never again shall I see them, or the fourteenth century church by the lakeside. I shall never hear the divine chime of its large silver bell. Our Castillo Rigolini on the hill looks like a castle of the moors ... The green fields of Umbria and the slender River Dora flowing through the vineyards ... I have started writing nonsense again.

Sitting at the entrance of the cave, I have been watching the countless stars for the last time. I remember St Franco's prayer to the Sun,

> *I pray to thee, my Lord, for blowing the wind and for calming the storm,*
> *I pray to thee for the earth, for the blue clouds and the sky,*
> *I pray to thee for the stars, for good times and bad, for the demise of this body.*

Another thing. Five large diamonds are kept in my boots. It is for you, my unknown traveller friend.

Please do not deny me my last request. May Mother Mary bless you.

Commander Attilio Gatti
1880, possibly the month of March

Unfortunate young man!

All of thirty years have passed since his death. In these thirty years, perhaps no one had come this way. Even if someone did, he had not entered the cave. It took such a long time for his letter to reach another human being.

After going through the letter, Shankar was convinced that the cave described in Attilio Gatti's letter was none other than the one in which he had nearly lost his life! Then he eagerly took the boots off the feet of the skeleton. Five large diamonds tumbled out of them. They were exactly like the pebbles he had collected in the dark cave for marking his way, one of which was still with him. He had seen thousands of these pebbles under the water of that dark river and on its shores! It was beyond his imagination that he had unexpectedly stumbled upon the very diamond reserve for which Alvarez and he had, for six months, searched desperately in the forests of the Richtersveldt Mountains. Neither could he comprehend that such an abundance of diamonds could be strewn around like ordinary pebbles! If he knew, he would have brought loads of them with him.

But what was worse, he had not noted down the location of the reserve. He had not even left any sign that could help him reach the place a second time. He had no idea where exactly he had found that cave by sheer chance. It was most unlikely that he would be able to locate it again. This young man also did not draw a map of the place, but that was understandable, he was grievously hurt shortly after discovering the deposit. Perhaps he had the skills to find the place even without maps, but Shankar had no such skills.

Suddenly, Shankar remembered what Alvarez had told him before his death: "Let's go, Shankar. An enormous treasure is lying in that cave. Can't you see? I see it clearly!"

Shankar buried the skeleton inside the cave. He broke the barrel, took two pieces of wood, and made a cross by fixing them with a rusty nail. He put the cross on the grave. He knew nothing more about the rituals of Christian burial. He prayed to god to grant peace to the soul of this young man.

All this took almost one full day. He rested for the night and started off the next morning. He took the letter and the diamonds carefully. A gloomy thought came to his mind. Whoever went in search of that cursed diamond reserve did not return alive. Attilio Gatti and his companions died, Jim Carter died, Diego Alvarez died. In all probability, many others had perished too. Possibly, it was his turn next. He too would breathe his last in this dreary desert, like that brave Italian sailor.

THIRTEEN

As the desert caught fire in the afternoon sun, Shankar took shelter behind a mound. The thermometer showed a hundred and thirty five degrees. No man of flesh and blood could walk in that heat. Perhaps he could have reached the civilized world if there was a way bypassing this ghastly desert! He dreaded the desert. He knew the Kalahari was the haunt of huge lions. But he had a gun and he was not afraid of facing a lion alone. What he was afraid of was the Demoness of Thirst. He had no defence against her. There was no escape from the agony of thirst. In the afternoon, twice he saw mirages. He had been in the desert for quite some time by then, but he had not come across the fantastic vision earlier, he had only read about it. He saw mirages twice, once in the north-east which was more vivid, and the second time in the south-east. Both the mirages were similar – they looked like a mosque or church with a big dome surrounded by date palms and a large body of water in the front.

By evening, Shankar saw cloud-like mountains in the horizon. He could not believe his eyes. Only one mountain range could be seen from here – the Chimanimani range on the borders of southern Rhodesia. He could not believe he was about to cross the immense Kalahari desert on foot! Oh god! Is this yet another mirage?

But as he continued walking till ten o'clock in the night, the contours of the mountain remained equally clear in the moonlight. Mirages are not seen in moonlight. He knelt down to thank god.

Was there still hope for him then! He was the owner of the largest diamond reserve in the world. He had earned his rights by tremendous suffering and fortitude. If only he could return alive to the lap of his poor motherland!

After two days, he reached the foothills of the mountain. Now, he was face to face with yet another hurdle. He had to either cross the mountain or walk at least twenty five miles through the desert to go around the mountain. Shankar hated the idea of walking any further in the desert. He decided to climb over.

By doing so, he tempted fate. It proved to be a colossal blunder. He forgot it was not a mean task to climb a high mountain, particularly when he was exhausted and weak due to lack of food and water. It was as difficult as crossing the Richtersveldts. In fact it was more difficult because then he was with Alvarez. Here, he was all alone.

Shankar underestimated his task. As a result, he reached

the jaws of death while crossing the Chimanimani. Even while crossing the burning Kalahari, he had not seen death from such close quarters.

The jungles on the Chimanimani were not too thick. Shankar climbed to quite a height on the first day. Then he reached a place from where he could not climb any more. Neither could he find the path by which he had reached that point. He felt he had moved away by at least thirty degrees from the point where he had started climbing at the foothills. He could not figure out how he deviated from the original direction so much. But he pegged away all the same. He went from one point to another, climbing up for some time and then scuttling down. He tried to move in the right direction by observing the sun, but he did not understand why it took so long to cover a distance of seven to eight miles.

On the third day, there was a new problem. The previous day he had been hurt in the leg when a loose boulder rolling down the hill had hit him. At that time, he had not felt much pain, but that morning, he was unable to stand up. His left knee was swollen. It was impossible to climb the mountain in this condition. He had collected water from a stream while coming up and he was still managing with that water. He had to wait there till his knee was better. Though he couldn't go far, he forced himself to move around a little in search of food and water. In a way, he was lucky as that part of the mountain was relatively flat.

Such hazards are quite common while climbing mountains far away from human habitation. Even European mountaineers could have faced similar situations. But Shankar could not take any more of this punishment. There was, he felt, some problem with his heart – it pounded heavily against his ribs if he walked even a short distance. He was completely worn out due to extreme fatigue, anxiety, poor food and more often, lack of food.

On the fourth day, totally exhausted, he took shelter under a tree. He had run out of food the previous day. Although he had a rifle, he did not get an animal within its shooting range. In the afternoon he was delighted to see an antelope, but his rifle was then fifty yards away, propped up against a tree. The antelope fled when he went to get the gun. There was a little water in his canteen, but he was not in a condition to climb down to the spring and fetch more. The swelling in his knee had increased and the pain was severe. He could hardly walk.

As the air was extremely dry, with no moisture in it, Shankar could see up to a long distance. There were blue mountains on the horizon on almost all sides. Towards the west, the flat Kalahari stretched out till the horizon. To his south was what he thought to be the Wahakoohok Mountain and behind it, the Paul Kruger Mountain range, seen like low clouds. Nothing much could be seen in the direction of Salisbury. A peak of the Chimanimani range blocked that side.

That afternoon, Shankar saw vultures flying in the sky above. He had never ever been so frightened. He felt they were telling him his time was running out. Did they know they were going to get their victim soon?

It was freezing cold. Shankar collected some dry twigs and leaves and lit a fire. The night was dark, nothing could be seen beyond the small glimmer of the fire.

An animal came and crouched down, almost merging with the darkness. It was an African hunting dog. Then a second one came and then a third … As the night progressed there were ten or twelve of them. They were waiting in the darkness for something, apparently with eternal patience.

It was such an unholy sight!

Shankar's blood chilled with fear. Was he really at the doorsteps of death? Would he too fail to return alive from the Richtersveldt with its diamonds?

The irony was that he had a fortune in his backpack. Even if he ignored the diamond reserve, the diamonds he had with him were worth not less than two to three lakhs of rupees. If only he could reach his poor village with such enormous riches. He could change the lives of many a poor man, he could pay for the wedding of many a young girl, could help many helpless old people.

But there was no point in dreaming about the impossible. He wanted to enjoy the beauty of the starry sky and the wonderful night, like his Italian predecessor, Attilio Gatti. Before his death he too wanted to observe the solemn, silent beauty of this mountain and the desert far below. There was an invisible bond among all of them, Attilio Gatti, his companions, Jim Carter, Diego Alvarez and Shankar.

It was late in the night, the cold was severe. He noticed that the wild dogs had come closer. Their eyes glowed in the light of the fire. They fled when Shankar threw a piece of burning wood at them. They moved slowly and silently, with endless patience. Shankar felt they knew their victim was within grasp, there was no way they would lose him.

He knew it would be dangerous to sleep and wondered whether the pack of dogs would tear him apart even when he was alive. Although he was sick and exhausted, he had to stay awake. He could not afford the luxury of a nap. The dogs inched forward slowly ... they ran away when he threw a piece of burning twig. Two hyenas also joined them. Their eyes shone brightly in the dark.

What a terrible situation he was in. At a height of about three thousand feet in a desolate mountain far away from the civilized world, he was immobilized and surrounded by hyenas and a pack of fierce wild dogs, which were patiently waiting to tear him apart at the first opportunity. The night was dark and all he had for protection was a small fire. Above him, in the cloudless, clear sky, innumerable stars shone like tiny electric lights ...

At the same time, he reflected, he was not dying a useless death after a bout of malaria in a village in Bengal. His death would be an honourable, valiant death. He has crossed the great Kalahari Desert on foot – all alone. The Chimanimani mountain will silently record the event as the death of a great traveller and explorer. After all, he has discovered a great diamond deposit. After Alvarez's death, he had come out of the confounding maze of that vast mountain forest. Now he was helpless, sick and immobilized. Even then, he was struggling, he had not given up. He was not a coward. Life and death depends on god's will, he couldn't help it if he died.

The long night was over and there was light in the east. The wild animals vanished from the scene. As the day wore on, the ruthless sun started burning all corners of the mountain. The vultures arrived as if on a cue. Some of them flew above his head, some waited patiently on the branches of trees or on boulders on the ground. They seemed to tell Shankar that they were not in a hurry, but at the same time, they put him on notice. They wouldn't let him slip out.

Shankar was not hungry, neither did he want to eat. But still he shot a vulture.

The sun was scalding and the rocks were so hot that he could not step on them. The terrain was like a desert with no food or water. He lighted a fire and started roasting the bird. Earlier too, while in the desert, he had eaten vulture meat. This was his only source of food. Today he was eating them, tomorrow they would eat his corpse.

Shankar's shadow fell on the ground. In that lonely mountain, Shankar's unsettled mind thought the shadow was a companion he had. He was perhaps becoming insane! A couple of times he started talking to his shadow, but the next moment he realized his mistake and checked himself.

Is he really going mad? Does he have fever? He was totally confused. Alvarez … the diamond reserve … mountains and mountains … the ocean of sand … Attilio Gatti … He had not slept last night … it was going to be dark soon. Now he would sleep for a while.

He came out of his trance on hearing a noise. He wondered what made such an unusual sound. He could not understand from where it came, but the clatter gradually became louder. Suddenly, looking at the sky, Shankar was dumbfounded. Something was flying over his head, making a terrible clatter.

Shankar recognized it as an aeroplane, he had seen its picture in books. When it was above his head, Shankar shouted, waved his shirt and a broken branch, but he could not draw the attention of the pilot. In no time the aeroplane vanished over the violet hills of the Paul Kruger range.

Shankar thought more planes might fly this way. It was a fascinating machine. He had not seen a plane in India.

He decided to light a fire with fresh leaves, which would make a lot of smoke. If the aeroplane flew this way again, the pilot would hopefully see him. The plane did him one favour, it drove away the vultures.

That day also was over. With darkness, Shankar's ordeal started all over again. It was a rerun of the previous night. The pack of African hunting dogs came and sat around him, away from the fire. Shankar did not know how to drive them away. He could not shoot them, he had only two cartridges left. He would have to starve if he ran out of bullets. He was going to die in any case, sooner or later, but he refused to give up.

But he had to use his gun. Before morning, the hyenas came and that gave courage to the dogs. They too came closer. They no longer ran away when Shankar threw burning wood at them.

Shankar dozed off for a moment. He woke up with a start to find that one of the hunting dogs had come dangerously close to him. He was afraid it would pounce upon him any moment. In a nervous reaction, he fired a shot.

The same thing was repeated after some time. The dogs had immense patience, they waited quietly.

With dawn, the animals vanished like a nightmare. The next moment Shankar fell asleep by the side of the fire.

He was awakened by a sound.

There had been a booming noise a little earlier. Shankar could hear a reverberation even after waking up.

Had he heard a gunshot? But that was impossible. How could there be another human being in this remote mountain? Shankar had only one cartridge left. He took a chance and fired a shot. In response, someone fired two shots.

Shankar was beside himself with excitement and joy, he forgot about his swollen knee, he forgot he could hardly walk. He had no cartridge left, he could not fire his gun again, but he shouted himself hoarse. He broke a branch from a tree and waived it. He frantically foraged for dry twigs to light a fire.

A survey team from the Kruger National Park was going from Kimberley to Cape Town. They had pitched camp on the north-eastern edge of the desert under the Chimanimani mountain. They had with them seven motor vehicles with caterpillar wheels. There were nine Europeans in the team besides African helpers and porters.

Four of them had climbed up to the lowest level of Chimanimani mountain in search of game. They were surprised to hear a rifle shot in that desolate, uninhabited forest. As there were no further shots, they went deeper into the forest to check what it was all about. Then they saw a thin, ghost-like figure with sunken eyes and dishevelled hair waving at them like a madman. He was wearing ragged European clothes.

They rushed towards Shankar. Shankar wanted to say many things at the same time and jabbered away, making little sense. They did not make head or tail of what he told them. They took him to their camp gently and carried his backpack. He was put on a bed.

It took quite some time for Shankar to recover. He was sick and completely worn out because of continuous starvation, worry, and from eating all sorts of things. He came down with high fever that night.

Unconscious with fever, he did not know when the vehicle carrying him left or when they reached Salisbury. He spent fifteen days in a Salisbury hospital in a critical condition. Then he recovered gradually and after about a month walked out of the hospital to stand on the main road.

FOURTEEN

Salisbury! It was a dream come true.

He was actually standing on the pavement of a modern city. There were tall buildings, banks and hotels. There were wide macadam roads, along the side of which electric trams plied, Zulu riksha-pullers were pulling rikshas, vendors were selling newspapers. All this seemed absolutely new to him.

He had returned to civilization, but he was penniless. He did not have money for buying even a cup of tea. He was delighted to see an Indian shop nearby. He had not seen another Indian in a long time. The shopkeeper was a Memon Muslim, a wholesale dealer of soaps and perfumes. His store was fairly large. He was sympathetic and understood Shankar's situation. He gave Shankar two pounds and asked him to meet an important Indian merchant.

Shankar took the money and told him, "Thank you very much for these two pounds, I am borrowing this money, I will return this as soon as I can."

He came out of the shop. Across the road, he found an Indian restaurant. He could not resist the temptation of good food. He ate puris, kachouris, mutton cutlet, halwa and cakes to his heart's content and spent one pound in the process. He also had two or three cups of coffee.

There was an old newspaper on his table. A bold headline in the newspaper said,

· Strange Experience of the National Park Survey Team
A Dying Indian Found in the Desert
His Fascinating Adventures

The paper carried an entirely imaginary story attributed to him. Shankar had never told such a story to anyone. Shankar's photograph also figured in the paper.

The newspaper was the *Salisbury Daily Chronicle*. He went to the newspaper's office and introduced himself. In a short while a small crowd gathered around him. They told him that reporters had lost his trail and could not find him although they were very interested in his story. Shankar earned fifty pounds by telling them his experience in the Chimanimani mountain and allowing them to photograph him. From this, he returned the two pounds to the kind Muslim gentleman.

He wrote an article on the volcano for the paper. He christened it Mount Alvarez. Not everyone believed his story of a volcanic eruption in the unknown forests of Central Africa, but some did. In the article, he did not give the slightest hint about the diamond reserve. If he wrote about it, thousands of people would rush to search for it.

Later, he went to a bookstore and purchased a number of books and periodicals. He had not read anything in a long time. In the evening he saw a movie. At night, he lay down under an electric lamp on a comfortable bed in his hotel room, and occasionally looked at the Prince Albert Victor Street below, while reading a book. Trams and rikshas were passing by, a bell was ringing in the Indian coffee shop, once in a way a motor car passed. Another picture floated before his eyes – A fire in front of him, and hunting dogs and hyenas surrounding him, their eyes shining like fireballs in the dark.

He wondered which of these was real! The dreadful night in the Chimanimani mountain, or the present…

In the meantime, Shankar had become a famous man in Salisbury.

The lobby of his hotel was always full of reporters. The newspaper people came to tie up contracts with him for publishing his travelogues. Photographers came to take his pictures.

He informed the Italian Consul General about Commander Attilio Gatti. By searching old papers in his office, it was found that an aristocratic Italian by the name of Attilio Gatti had been shipwrecked off the coast of Portuguese West Africa in August 1879. Somehow it was also known that he had reached the shore, but nothing was heard of him thereafter. His family was not only aristocratic, but also very rich. Till 1890 or '95, they were after their embassies in all the countries in East, West and South Africa. A reward was also announced for tracing him. They had given up the search after 1895.

With the help of the kind Indian trader he met on the first day, Shankar sold four diamonds to the biggest jeweller on Blackmoon Street, Rhydal & Moresby, for thirty two thousand and five hundred pounds. The jewellers were prepared to pay more for the two remaining gems, but Shankar did not sell them. He wanted to take them home and show them to his mother.

Blue sea.

Standing on the deck of a Bombay bound ship, Shankar watched the green coconut groves of Port Beira of Portuguese East Africa fading in the horizon as he recalled his adventures. This was how he had wanted to live his life, fully and vigorously. We measure a man by a wrong yardstick, his age. In the last one and a half years, Shankar had gathered ten years of experience. He was not just another vagabond traveller any more, he was the co-discoverer of a living volcano. He was going to inform the whole word about Mount Alvarez. Now he was restless for his motherland, that wonderful place called Bharotborsho. He was eagerly waiting to see the tall pinnacle of the Rajabhai Tower of Bombay to announce the arrival of his motherland. After that, his green village in a corner of Bengal, redolent with the music of baul and keertan ... It would be spring in a few days' time. When his boat reaches the jetty of their village, their village path would be paved with sojne flowers and the bou-katha-kao would warble from their bokul tree.

Goodbye, friend Alvarez. I remember you more than anyone else at this happy moment, when I am on my way home. You are among those rare people who are the true citizens of the world, who consider the sky the roof over their head, and the whole world, a path beneath their feet. Bless me from your solitary home in the deep forest, I want to be like you, detached in happiness and serene in crisis. And as fearless.

Good bye, my friend Attilio Gatti, perhaps you were a friend in my previous life.

All of you together have taught me how true is that Chinese saying, It is much much better to be a piece of crystal and be shattered to pieces, than to remain static and contented like a tile on the roof.

He will have to return to Africa. Now, at this moment, he has to go home. He will spend some time in his own motherland. Then he will try to form a company in his country itself. He will return to explore the far away Richtersveldts for the diamond deposit – he will certainly find it again!

While he was in Salisbury, Shankar had met the curator of the South Rhodesian Museum, the famous zoologist Dr Fitzgerald, particularly to tell him about the bunip. A few days after reaching home, he received the following letter from Dr Fitzgerald.

The South Rhodesian Museum
Salisbury, Rhodesia, South Africa
January 12, 1911

Dear Mr Choudhuri,

I am writing this letter to fulfil my promise to you to let you know what I thought about your report of a strange three-toed monster in the wilds of the Richtersveldt Mountains. On looking up my files I find other similar accounts by explorers who had been to the region before you, specially by Robert McCulloch, the famous naturalist, whose report has not yet been published, owing to his sudden and untimely death last year. On thinking the matter over, I am inclined to believe that the monster you saw was nothing more than a species of anthropoid ape, closely related to the gorilla, but much bigger in size and more savage than the specimens found in the Ruwenzori and Virunga mountains. This species is becoming rarer and rarer every day, and such numbers as do exist are not easily to be got at on account of their shyness and the habit of hiding themselves in the depths of the high altitude rainforests of the Richtersveldt. It is only the very fortunate traveller who gets glimpses of them, and I should think that in meeting them he runs a risk proportionate to his good luck.

Congratulating you both on your luck and pluck.

I remain,
Yours sincerely,
(Sd)
J G Fitzgerald

Translator's Acknowledgements and Excuses

I was fortunate to reach this world well before the television did. For a child living in urban India in the fifties and sixties, sources of entertainment were rather scarce, if we go by the current connotations of the word. Movies were rare gusts of happiness restricted to *Ben Hur*s and *African Safari*s. Cricket used to be an annual affair accompanied by oranges and sandwiches, the everlasting memories of which are a Roy or a Contractor ducking away from Davidson bouncers. Primary schools were pretty much happier places those days, and used to be over at a decent ten thirty in the morning. My long and lonely afternoons were spent observing kites in the sky and on the earth, trans-continental journeys undertaken by huge armies of ants. And of course, reading books.

The world of books was infinitely more gorgeous than the real world around me, I could indulge in fascinating voyages in a planet created by Charles Dickens and Rider Haggard, Jules Verne and Robert Louis Stevenson, Sukumar Ray and Bibhutibhushan ...

And in this treasure-trove, one gem to which I would return again and again was *Chander Pahad*. On the surface, it is an adventure story, but like any other great work of literature, it also tells us a few basic things about humankind. The underlying splendour of *The Mountain of the Moon* is much more significant than its apparent beauty, which of course, is great. Perhaps because of this, the few geographical and other inconsistencies that we come across in the novella really do not matter. On the contrary, it is amazing how the author could give such graphic details of the flora and fauna of the African continent, considering that the novella was first published in 1937 and its author never left the shores of India.

Although I loved *Chander Pahad* since my childhood, the thought of translating it had never occurred to me. I strayed into the field of literary translations largely because of the inspiration and prodding from my friend

Basu Bimochan Bhattacharya. But for him, this masterpiece by Bibhutibhushan would have been translated by someone else.

The author's son, Shri Taradas Banerjee kindly gave me permission to publish this translation, for which I am indebted to him. Shri Banerjee, an authority on Bibhutibhushan, has been exceedingly helpful to me throughout the work.

This was my first translation and I was unsure about the quality of the work (with good reasons to be, someone might say). Fortunately, I rediscovered my high school English teacher, Shri Suprabhat Chakraborty at a school reunion. With much apprehension, I requested him to go through the manuscript. And for the first time in my life, Sir returned my work without devastating red marks. His words of encouragement were a huge bonus. The manuscript was also checked by Ms Arunima Pal, to whom I am grateful. And I thank Ms Arundhuti Banerjee for transliteration of the Portuguese words used in the original in Bangla script.

My niece, Divyangana, daughter Sohini and son Ritwik have helped me to make my prose less stodgy and more appropriate for the readers whom Bibhutibhushan had in mind. They have been a great help.

It was a pleasure to work with the Katha team. They have added much value to my work and polished the rough edges, the least of which were orthographic inconsistencies.

Thank you all!

Kolkata   Santanu Sinha Chaudhuri
25 July 2003

Biographical Notes

Bibhutibhushan Bandopadhyay (1894-1950), a schoolteacher and a prolific writer, is noted for his depiction of the beauty of rural life in Bengal and Bihar. He has nearly two hundred published works to his credit – seventeen novels and twenty collections of short stories, including *Aporajito, Aranyak, Icchamati* and *Asani Sanket*. His greatest work, and one that brought him fame, is *Pather Panchali*. He was posthumously awarded the Rabindra Memorial Prize in 1951 for his novel *Icchamati*. Some of his stories and novels, including *Pather Panchali* and *Asani Sanket*, have been adapted into films by the well-known filmmaker Satyajit Ray.

An avid worshipper of nature, Bibhutibhushan was a pioneer of conservation of environment. He wanted to save what he loved. His interests in life were varied. Part of his personal library containing books on astronomy, physics, botany, world literature, anthropology, philosophy and the earth sciences still exists.

Santanu Sinha Chaudhuri is interested in reading, travelling, photography, music and furniture designing. Translating Bangla fiction into English, for him, is more than a serious hobby. Besides *The Mountain of the Moon*, he has translated Shirshendu Mukhopadhyay's *Manab Jamin* and *The Ghost from the Gosai Garden*, a novella for children. He has also translated a collection of short stories by Dibyendu Palit.

Suddhasattwa Basu, a renowned illustrator, has many children's books as well as magazines and paintings to his credit. He has also worked on animation films for television. His latest book, *The Song of the Scarecrow* – for which he won the ChitraKatha Award 2003 – has received an honourable mention at the Biennial of Illustration Bratislava in 2003.

ABOUT KATHA

India has always been a land of storytellers. Over the centuries, we have honed the fine art of telling the short story – be it in our epics, our mythologies, our folktales or in our more recent writings. Told by traditional Katha vachaks, village storytellers and one's favourite grandmother, we have all heard stories that have taught us our values, our morals, our culture. "Katha" or the narrative is a special legacy that continues to exist in our country as a rich and fascinating tradition, moving with grace and felicity from the oral traditions to the written texts, from the heard word to the read.

We at Katha endeavour to spread the joy of reading, knowing, and living amongst adults and children, the common reader and the neo-literate. Katha has striven to establish a code of excellence in all that it does, to enhance the quality of life in every project it has attempted.

Katha's main objective is **to enhance the pleasures of reading for children and adults,** for experienced readers as well as for those who are just beginning to read. And, inter alia, to –

- Stimulate an interest in lifelong learning that will help the child grow into a confident, self-reliant, responsible and responsive adult.
- Help break down gender, cultural and social stereotypes.
- Encourage, foster excellence, and applaud quality literature and translations in and between the various Indian languages.

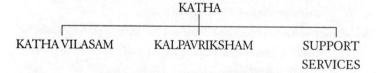

KATHA VILASAM: The Story Research and Resource Centre was created in September 1989 with the following main purposes:
- To help capacity build in writers, translators and editors. To organize and promote, wherever required, the study of those subjects through lectures, demonstrations/workshops etc.

- To offer a decentralized research and a centralized documentation service on Indian literature, focusing on short fiction. The idea is to collect and have for larger use research papers, writings and other forms of scholarship on writers and writings.
- To publish quality translations of good writings from the various Indian languages, in English.

These goals have crystallized in the development of the following areas of activities:

- **Katha Books**: Publishing of Quality Translations
- **Academic Publishing Programme:** Books for teaching of translation and Indian fiction
- **Applauding Excellence**: The Katha Awards for fiction, translation, editing
- **Kathakaar**: The Centre for Children's Literature
- **Katha Barani**: The Translation Resource Centre
- **Katha Sethu**: Building bridges between India and the outside world
  - **The Katha Translation Exchange Programme**
  - **Translation Contests**
- **Kanchi**: Katha National Institute of Translation was started in 1994 with the Vak Initiative for enhancing the pool of translators between the various bhashas.
  - **Katha Academic Centres.** In various universities across the country
  - **The Faculty Enhancement programme.** Workshops, seminars, discussions
  - **Sishya:** Katha Clubs in colleges; workshops, certificate courses, events and contests
  - **The Katha Internship programme** for students from outside India
  - **Storytellers Unlimited**: Stotytelling – the Art and Craft
  - **KathaRasa**: Performances, Art Fusion, events. Katha Centre Activities

KALPAVRIKSHAM: The Centre for Sustainable Learning was created in September 1989 with the following main purposes:

- To foster quality education for children from nonliterate families that is relevant and fun
- To develop teaching/learning materials that see the story as the basis, for fostering lifelong learning skills and knowledge in our children that will make classroom teaching rememberable and understandable.
- To find, foster, and applaud good teaching of our children, through inservice and preservice training.

These goals crystallized in the development of the following areas of activities:

- **Katha Khazana**
  - **Katha Student Support Centre.**
  - **Katha Public School**
  - **Katha School of Entrepreneurship**
  - **KITES.** Katha Information Technology and eCommerce School
  - **Iccha Ghar. The Intel Computer Clubhouse @ Katha**
  - **Hamara Gaon.** Community revitalization and economic resurgence.
  - **The Mandals**: Maa, Bapu, Balika, Balak, Danadini
  - **The Clubs:** Inducement to activity clubs like Gender Club, Mensa Club etc.
  - **KathaRasa,** Artistic education, performances, events.
- **Shakti Khazana**: Skills upgradation. Income generation activities. The Khazana Coop.
- **Kalpana Vilasam:** Regular research and development of teaching/learning materials, curricula, syllabi, content
  - **Teacher training.**
  - **TaQeEd — The Teachers Alliance for Quality eEducation.**
- **Tamasha'S World!**
  - **Tamasha!** the Children's magazine
  - *Dhammakdhum!*
  - *www.tamasha.org*
  - **ANU — Animals, Nature and YOU!**

BE A FRIEND OF KATHA!

If you feel strongly about Indian literature, you belong with us! KathaNet, an invaluable network of our friends, is the mainstay of all our translation-related activities. We are happy to invite you to join this ever-widening circle of translation activists. Katha, with limited financial resources, is propped up by the unqualified enthusiasm and the indispensable support of nearly 5000 dedicated women and men.

We are constantly on the lookout for people who can spare the time to find stories for us, and to translate them. Katha has been able to access mainly the literature of the major Indian languages. Our efforts to locate resource people who could make the lesser-known literatures available to us have not yielded satisfactory results. We are specially eager to find Friends who could introduce us to Bhojpuri, Dogri, Kashmiri, Maithili, Manipuri, Nepali, Rajasthani and Sindhi fiction.

Do write to us with details about yourself, your language skills, the ways in which you can help us, and any material that you already have and feel might be publishable under a Katha programme. All this would be a labour of love, of course! But we do offer a discount of 20% on all our publications to Friends of Katha.

Write to us at –

Katha
A-3 Sarvodaya Enclave
Sri Aurobindo Marg   Call us at: 2686-8193, 2652-1752
New Delhi 110 017   or E-mail us at: info@katha.org

Help shape a child's future!

Doctor, engineer, policewoman,
mechanic, computer specialist ...
what will I be?

What happens when 1200 children, many of them working, 55 determined teachers and a whole community come together? Sheer magic!

You'll find this excitement in the air when you enter the brick low-cost building that houses Katha-Khazana. Children learning by doing, women entrepreneurs at work, people from the community taking a keen interest in the lives of their children.

The children and women of Govindpuri, a large slum cluster of more than 100,000 people, have come a long way in more than twelve years Katha has been working with them. But there are excitements ahead. Small but sure steps towards self-confidence, self-reliance touched by the power of self-esteem, the craving for knowledge. Many of the children who come to us are working to support their families, see how far they've travelled! Doing their BAs and BComs from Delhi's colleges ... dreaming of becoming doctors and engineers, computer specialists, catering managers, all entrepreneurs ... knowing that these dreams can come true!

You can be a special friend of
our children by sponsoring their
education at Katha.
Yes, I would like to sponsor

❑ Rs 350/- every month   ❑ Rs 2100/- for six months

❑ Rs 4200/- for one year   ❑ Rs 8400/- for two years

❑ Rs 12600/- for three years   or   ❑ Rs ..../- every .... years

[*350/- pays for the basic and computer education of one child for a month.]

Please prepare your cheque/DD in favour of Katha Resources to Educate a Child Fund. Visit us at www.katha.org to donate online.

Donations to Katha are exempted under sections 80 G (50%IT exemption) and 35 AC (100% IT exemption) of the IT Act 1961. Katha is also registered under FCRA and can receive donations in foreign currencies.